THE INVISIBLE WILD

NIKKI VAN DE CAR

RP|TEENS
PHILADELPHIA

This book is a work of fiction. Names, characters, places, and incidents are the product of the author's imagination or are used fictitiously. Any resemblance to actual events, locales, or persons, living or dead, is coincidental.

Text copyright © 2025 by Nikki Van De Car
Cover illustration copyright © 2025 by Carolina Rodriguez Fuenmayor
Cover copyright © 2025 by Hachette Book Group, Inc.

Hachette Book Group supports the right to free expression and the value of copyright. The purpose of copyright is to encourage writers and artists to produce the creative works that enrich our culture.

The scanning, uploading, and distribution of this book without permission is a theft of the author's intellectual property. If you would like permission to use material from the book (other than for review purposes), please contact permissions@hbgusa.com. Thank you for your support of the author's rights.

Running Press Teens
Hachette Book Group
1290 Avenue of the Americas, New York, NY 10104
www.runningpresskids.com
@runningpresskids

First Edition: May 2025

Published by Running Press Teens, an imprint of Hachette Book Group, Inc. The Running Press Teens name and logo are trademarks of Hachette Book Group, Inc.

The Hachette Speakers Bureau provides a wide range of authors for speaking events. To find out more, go to www.hachettespeakersbureau.com or email HachetteSpeakers@hbgusa.com.

Running Press books may be purchased in bulk for business, educational, or promotional use. For more information, please contact your local bookseller or the Hachette Book Group Special Markets Department at Special.Markets@hbgusa.com.

The publisher is not responsible for websites (or their content) that are not owned by the publisher.

Print book interior illustrations: Getty Images
Print book cover and interior design by Frances J. Soo Ping Chow

Library of Congress Cataloging-in-Publication Data has been applied for.

ISBNs: 978-0-7624-8706-6 (hardcover), 978-0-7624-8707-3 (ebook)

Printed in Indiana, USA

LSC-C

Printing 1, 2025

TO THOSE OF US

WHO SEE THE THINGS

THAT MIGHT NOT BE THERE,

AND WHO FEEL LOST

EVEN WHEN WE AREN'T,

NOT AT ALL

PREFACE

The thing about stories is, they are always true.

Even when they are contradictory, they are true, because they were told, and told again, over and over, until they created an indelible mark on the infinite canvas of time, like a kūkaenēnē ink stamp on kapa cloth.

This is just one of those stories.

According to legend, when the kanaka ʻōiwi sailed over two thousand miles across untraveled seas to the most remote island chain in the world, they encountered another people living there.

They were two to three feet tall, squat and strong. They wore what might be considered angry resting faces, but they were good and kind and bothered no one without cause. They were intelligent, industrious, and organized, and they worked smoothly together as a community. They played in the same way that they worked, together and with great skill, diving from cliffs into the sea, singing, and telling stories. They were once so numerous that they could stand two abreast and pass rocks hand to hand from Makaweli to Wailua on the island of Kauaʻi, a distance of twenty-five miles.

They lived in caves and ate the fruits of the forest. They were skilled laborers and built temples, roads, waterways, fishponds, and canoes—and would always, always complete their work in a single night. They were never seen in the daytime. Was this because they were invisible by day? Or did they fear the light?

But when the Hawaiians came, the chieftains of these fierce people feared the changes they brought. On the night of a full moon, they called all men and their firstborn sons and ordered them to leave Hawai'i. Any younger children, and any relationships they had with the newcomers, would have to be abandoned.

Some refused to leave their Hawaiian wives and part-Hawaiian children. They did not join the exodus and instead hid to remain behind with their families. In the early 1800s, Kaua'i chief Kaumuali'i took a census of his people—and sixty-five of his two thousand subjects were all that remained of the original people of Hawai'i.

They were the menehune.

PROLOGUE

Whenever I go to the beach, I swim straight out until I am past everyone else in the water, until all I can see is blue, uninterrupted by people. Then I dive down, kicking my feet up out of the water, trying to propel myself to the seafloor, my ears protesting.

When I touch the sandy floor, rippling like a tiny mountain range, I look up. It's blurry. Our eyes are not meant for this underwater world. But the barrier between the worlds, the skin of the ocean—that is always perfectly clear. The thin, untouchable but unmistakable separation between two neighboring but never-mixing worlds. I kick off the bottom and soar up and out of the water, my chest and arms breaching like a humpback whale, bursting through that barrier.

It's easily broken, like it's not even there.

And what I've learned over the course of this past crazy month is that the invisible wild, the line between what's real and what isn't, is just as thin, just as easily broken, as the skin of the ocean.

CHAPTER ONE

I HONESTLY COULDN'T BELIEVE MY MOM LET ME drive on my own. I had my permit, but I'd failed the road test (apparently parallel parking is a nonnegotiable skill), and technically, I still wasn't allowed to operate a vehicle without a licensed adult present. Now, most people ignore that rule, but my mom was Victoria Arruda, and if Safety was her middle name, Law-Abiding was her other one, and ordinarily, no amount of whining and/or well-reasoned litigating would ever make her bend.

Turns out all that needed to happen to change her mind was for my sister to decide to get married.

The wedding was in one month, and we still had So Much To Do. To give herself more time to prepare, Mom had taken time off from the law practice she shared with my dad—which was basically unheard of—and one of the many things on her to-do list was to clean out all the crap we'd been storing in the garage. I mean, I thought that was basically what garages were for, but she said, "It's a *wedding*, Emma. It's *your sister's wedding.*"

"Yeah, but they're not getting married in the garage, right?"

Mom stood, dislodging the not-very-orderly piles of snorkels, fins, old dog toys, and random tools my dad had misplaced over the years. "Emma. A wedding is a big deal. I'm asking you to help me, but if you feel that your sister doesn't deserve your love and support, then that is your decision."

Yeah, so anyway, obviously I spent the rest of the afternoon pointlessly cleaning out the garage just to ease my mom's anxieties about the wedding. Absolutely the best use of everyone's time.

When at last we'd finished, the piles of stuff that weren't destined for the town dump needed to be taken to Cooper Center for donation. Cooper Center was the town community center, the place where the local hula halau practiced and the quilting club stitched while bitching. There was a farmers' market on Sundays and a swap meet every other Saturday. It had a playground and a skate park, and right now the most important thing about it was that it took just about any random crap you wanted to get rid of. And we had a carload of random crap.

By the time I'd finished loading the car, Mom was elbow-deep in retiling the shower (again, they were not getting married in the shower, but there was clearly no point in telling my mom that), and Dad was at work, so that left me to handle the drop-off. I grabbed the keys and left before she could change her mind.

Cooper Center was all of half a mile away, but this was my chance to show her—and myself—that I was more than capable of driving.

"Howzit, Emma? You need help?"

"No need, Auntie, I got it." Auntie Mele sat where she always did, where she could keep one eye on the door and another on the back of the store. She was not my aunt, specifically—she was more like everyone's aunt. She was in charge of sorting the donations and putting them out for sale, but her real job was knowing exactly what every single one of the 2,500 people living in Volcano, Hawaiʻi, was doing at any given moment. I leaned over and gave her a kiss on her cheek.

"How are the wedding preparations coming along? You going to be ready in time?"

"Absolutely. We're almost done," I lied.

"And your sister's girlfriend? She knows what she's getting into, marrying a local girl?"

I grinned. "You know Puʻulena. She's got a way of getting what she wants. And anyway, Naomi loves her. They're great together."

"Yeah, but still." Auntie Mele was skeptical. "A mainland girl . . ."

"It'll be fine, Auntie," I said patiently. "They've been together for years."

I continued to fend off Auntie Mele's concern/curiosity as I went back and forth from the car unloading old clothes, formerly beloved stuffed animals, random mismatched plates, and a truly hideous painting my dad got as payment for services rendered instead of, you know, actual money.

"All pau," I said. "Do you need help with anything, Auntie?"

She smiled up at me and patted my arm. "You're a good girl. No, I'm fine. Actually, try wait...." She thought for a moment. "Can you get me another ball of yarn? I'm almost pau with this one." She held up the mostly finished crocheted blanket spread over her lap. "What do you think?"

"Oh, it's so pretty, Auntie!" Auntie Mele had crocheted a blanket for every baby born in town in the past twenty years. Volcano was a small town, but still, that was a lot of blankets. "Where's the yarn?"

The yarn was tucked way up on a shelf in the back room, behind a box of old shoes and another box of mismatched LEGOs. I gave the yarn to Auntie Mele in exchange for a hug and a promise that I would say hi to my mom for her.

Feeling accomplished, I was headed back toward the car when I spotted, ugh, a ceramic mug that I was supposed to have dropped off. It must have fallen out of the bag, and the handle had broken off. Even Cooper Center wouldn't take it as a donation now. Annoyed at myself, I kicked it out of sight, into the woods, then climbed into the car and put it in reverse.

Here's the thing: I didn't much care for reversing. I couldn't get a handle on the whole process of turning the wheel to the right to go left. In retrospect, that issue was probably at the core of my parallel-parking difficulties. Obviously, this would all be a moot point if my parents would let me drive the Prius, with its rear camera and self-parking features, but I'd been unequivocally informed that this was not an option.

Biting my lip, I put my arm up on the passenger seat of our much older RAV4, stepped gingerly on the gas, and let the car roll slowly backward.

A shape fluttered across my vision, like a bat or a bird or something, but way too big to be either. I gasped and slammed on the brake. Except in my panic, I didn't slam on the brake; I slammed on the gas and, as the car lurched backward, I screamed.

"What the hell do you think you're doing?"

I slammed my foot down on the brake—the actual brake this time—and looked back again. There was no bird. Instead, there was a really pissed-off boy.

"I'm sorry!" I yelled. "I . . . I thought I saw something. Sorry!"

The boy walked over to my window, and I cringed. The near accident had attracted the attention of the kids at the skate park, and they were headed our way.

5

"You *thought* you saw something?" the boy said.

"Do you think maybe you *did* see something, and it was me?"

"No, it wasn't, it . . ." I took a breath. "I'm really sorry, okay? Anyway, I didn't actually hit you."

"Oh, cool, well, in that case, it's all good!" he snapped.

"Eh, brah, you okay?" Ikaika came jogging up, his skateboard under his arm. "Emma, what are you doing? You finally get your license?"

I glared at him. "Shut up." Really, nothing like having your ex around to witness your humiliation.

Ikaika gave me a look. "Get out of the car; I'll back it up for you."

"I don't need—"

"Yes, you do," the boy said.

"He's right." Ikaika smirked. "You don't want to make us look bad in front of kids from Hilo, do you?"

"Oh, please," I scoffed as I climbed out of the car. "Like Hilo's some big city."

"Hey, at least we have a grocery store. And people that know how to drive," the boy said. "Volcano is a nothing town with a stupid name."

We were on the slope of Mauna Loa, a literal volcano, so really it was a very sensible name, if a little on the nose. But I didn't bother answering the Hilo boy, because what was the point? I had dealt with his type before. He was probably exactly like Ikaika—tan, cute, hair bleached at the tips because of time spent in the sun, surfed so thought he was a badass, and would grow up and never go any farther away than Honolulu.

    I could deal with Ikaika because we'd grown up together. There was a code of being nice to your own when you lived in a town so small it was actually called a village. There had to be. Ikaika and I had dated for only a few months last year, and that probably wouldn't even have happened at all except neither of us had a lot of other options. In a larger town, we probably would have hated each other, but instead we messed around for a while, and when that didn't last for obvious reasons including but not limited to having zero things in common, we stayed friendly. Hard to be anything else with someone you have to see all the time.

    But I had no such code with Hilo, and no patience for boys like him.

    All the same, I tugged uncomfortably at my T-shirt, filthy from garage cleaning, and had to restrain myself from smoothing down my hair, which tended to get giant in humidity. And it was always humid here.

    Hilo frowned at the phrase printed on my shirt. "What does that mean?"

    I crossed my arms over my chest. Why were T-shirts always designed in such a way that the words stretched right across your boobs? "It's Latin."

    "Latin? What's it mean?" he repeated.

    "*Caesar non supra grammaticos.* The emperor is not above the grammarians," I said.

    Hilo looked at me blankly.

"I like grammar," I explained.

He looked blanker still.

"Emma, you coming or what?" Ikaika stood next to my car, holding the door open for me. I walked away from Hilo and climbed in with a muttered thanks. As I slammed the door, I heard Ikaika ask Hilo if he wanted to skate over to the general store to grab a musubi.

"They're all sold out," I hollered. "You know my uncle Danny never makes enough."

"Tell him to quit making hard-boiled eggs and make some more Spam musubi!" Ikaika yelled back. "Nobody likes those!"

CHAPTER TWO

LIKE I SAID, IT WAS *HALF A MILE* FROM COOPER Center to my house, but I somehow managed to get in another almost-accident.

This one wasn't my fault, though, and what I almost hit wasn't anything imaginary, either. It was Snookie. Snookie was a dog, the ugliest dog you've ever seen. He was a brindle and looked like a pit bull had gotten busy with an Akita and it hadn't worked out at all, like when two gorgeous movie stars have really weird-looking kids. But what made Snookie truly noteworthy was his durability. Everyone in town had hit Snookie at least once—one time, my uncle hit him twice in the same day. (Not my uncle who owns the general store. My other uncle, who's a mechanic.) Snookie was indestructible and knew it, and so he ran fearlessly at cars.

I should have been expecting Snookie—he was always running down to visit my dog, Mālie. Her name means "calm," but unfortunately, it wasn't accurate in her case. She was always jumping, and always trying to escape, sneaking out of our fenced-in yard with all the cunning and ingenuity of Harry Houdini. But we always knew where we would find her—holed up with Snookie, the love of her life.

I swerved into the ginger bushes alongside the road to avoid him, which I know you're not supposed to do, but at least ginger, with its smooth green leaves and soft branches, wouldn't scratch the car. What I didn't realize was that the tall stand of ginger was camouflaging the fact that the shoulder dropped down about a foot. The car lurched over, and I screamed and slammed on the brakes—really the brakes this time.

Snookie panted at me as he trotted past, his wiry tail wagging.

I put the car in reverse and tried to get it to hurl itself back up onto the road, but the right front tire wasn't going anywhere. I put my head down onto the wheel and tried not to cry. After a few shaky breaths, I turned off the car and climbed out to take a look. I struggled my way through the ginger, which was all tangled up around the front right tire, and squatted and half-heartedly tried pushing the car back up onto the road. I didn't really expect anything to happen—I'm not exactly Wonder Woman—but it was still worth a shot. Suddenly, I heard a rustling in the bushes behind me and turned, half expecting to see a feral pig or something. But there wasn't anything there.

At least nothing I could see. And yet, in the shadows beneath the trees, there was something. I peered into the brush, holding my breath. Was that a . . .

"Emma! What happened?"

I jumped and looked back to the road to see Uncle Mike—my mechanic uncle—leaning out the window of his truck with a horrified expression on his face.

I was so relieved my knees almost gave out. "Oh, Uncle Mike, I don't know—I swerved to avoid Snookie, but then the car fell off the road, and I can't get it back up and I should have been home already and I don't know what to do."

Uncle Mike had climbed out of his truck before I'd even finished speaking and was peering down at the right tire. "Yeah, I can fix that," he said.

I stood to the side, trying to be helpful but mostly getting in the way, as my uncle hooked a chain from his truck to the back of my car. He pulled it out, no trouble, and gave me a stern look. "Next time, hit the dog. Everybody else does."

I nodded emphatically. "Yep, got it. Only, Uncle . . . don't tell my mom, okay?"

He studied me for a moment, then sighed. "Fine. As long as you don't tell her you saw me. I'm supposed to go over to your house this afternoon to help hang twinkle lights in the yard, but I've got to go haul some wrecked cars out of Leilani Estates."

"Deal." I gave him a quick hug. He tried to fend me off as he always did—he was forever covered in grease and oil—but as always, I ignored him. Anyway, I could hardly get any dirtier.

He watched me drive down the road before getting back into his truck. I waved at him and took a deep breath. Crisis averted, now back to cleaning.

It just wasn't my day.

There is always someone worse off than you, I heard my mom say in my head, and while ordinarily that would make me bristle and feel defensive, in the moment, I realized she wasn't wrong. After all, there *were* a lot of people worse off than me, and as I glanced in the rearview mirror, the evidence of that was pretty obvious. A few years ago, an eruption at Puʻu Ōʻo had flowed underground through lava tubes for miles and miles, bypassing Volcano Village and everything in between, before fountaining in Leilani Estates, a subdivision down toward the coast. Or it had been a subdivision, anyway. Now a huge swath of it was just a field of black rock.

There were still some remains of houses and cars, partially burned or stranded in the middle of the lava field in a tiny little kīpuka.

It could just as easily have been us. And one day, it would be. There was nothing quite so arrogant as living in a town called Volcano and expecting it to be safe to do so. But in truth, nowhere was entirely safe, and everyone who lived on the Big Island understood that. We were all subject to Pele's choices. According to the whims of the goddess of the volcano, the island caught fire, burned, and grew a little larger. It healed, and the forest was reborn, but it could always catch fire again. It was a cycle we accepted, for the privilege of living here.

And it was different, somehow, from the horrific destruction of the wildfires on Maui. Those were caused by humans, by the heating of a planet, by the unmanaged invasive grasses. The drought and the answering surge in hurricanes were not part of the natural cycle of death and rebirth; the firestorm of Lāhainā was something we did to ourselves—or, more accurately, was something done to the people of Maui by a world unconcerned with the damage its choices wreaked.

When I pulled into the driveway at last, tires crunching over the gravel, the Prius was there, still warm from my dad's drive home. I tiptoed into the house, expecting to be yelled at for crashing the car, because invariably my parents knew when I'd screwed up, like they had magic powers or something. But instead, my dad handed me a package as he shrugged off his jacket and loosened his tie. Normally, it'd be Aloha Friday and he could get away with just a moderately threadbare aloha shirt, but I guess he had court today. I couldn't help grinning at the tie. It was his fish tie, the one my sister got him for Christmas a few years ago. When his jacket was buttoned it looked like a normal tie, but when it was unbuttoned, it was clearly a fish.

"Your order from Basically Books arrived," Dad said.

I gave a squee and clutched it, delighted. I was currently in the middle of reading *Wuthering Heights*, as I tended to every few months, but this was a *new* book, a book I hadn't read yet. I held it in front of me with a mixture of elation and suspicion. Because yay, new book! But also, I didn't trust books I hadn't read yet. I'd encountered too many that didn't honor the contract we'd made together when I opened them—a contract promising a pleasing reading experience—and had led me in a direction that was wildly unsatisfying.

I'd learned that there was really only one solution to this problem. After reading the first ten to twenty pages, enough to get a sense of who the characters were and what the main conflict might be, I flipped to the last few pages and took a quick peek. Did everything work out? For instance, if the love interest at the end was different from who it appeared it would be at the beginning, then that was very good information for me to have at the outset, and I would resolve to like that other character instead.

I was sitting at the kitchen table doing exactly that when my mom walked in to start cooking dinner. "Emma! Stop that! I can't *believe* you do that—just read the book and find out what happens the regular way!"

"Nope, can't do it," I said, flipping back to the beginning. "I've been hurt too many times."

My dad choked on a laugh as Mom sighed, exasperated. "I can't watch," she said.

I stood up and patted her on the shoulder. "I will remove my offensive reading habits from your presence, Mom." She made a face and blew me a kiss as I retreated to my room.

It was small and cluttered with half-finished craft projects and overstuffed journals, the walls decorated with posters of vintage book covers and an annoyingly gorgeous painting my best friend had given me. I ignored the piles of laundry on the floor, obviously, and flopped down onto my bed, opening the book with a sigh of contentment. It felt like only minutes later that my mom hollered at me to come to the table for dinner.

When I came into the kitchen, my parents were deep in conversation at the table and barely noticed me. I went over to the stove to serve myself—ooh, chicken katsu tonight, yum—and dumped an excessive amount of shoyu over my rice.

"Apparently, the permits got pushed through under the table, no community notification or anything," Dad said.

"But how can they do that?" my mom asked. "How can they just skip the entire process?"

"You know how," he said, and I could hear a hint of anger in his voice. It took a lot to get my dad angry. "Pay the right people, make the right 'donations,' and suddenly the project is expedited."

"What project?" I asked, sliding into my chair.

My dad sighed. "You know that property up the back of Wright Road?"

I knew the one he meant. It was twenty-five gorgeous acres and miraculously pristine. Unlike much of the land back there, it hadn't been cleared for pasture or crops, and there was almost no trace of invasives—the ginger hadn't touched it, nor had the destructive tibouchina or faya. It was all ʻōhiʻa trees with their gray-green leaves and startlingly red lehua blossoms, and ʻōlapa trees, whose mango-scented leaves fluttered in the wind, and hāpuʻu, the giant ferns that stood tall and proud, like a ceiling of interlocking umbrellas protecting the mosses and smaller ferns below.

It was magical. Theoretically, it had been for sale for many years, but whoever owned it was asking an absurd amount of money. (Not really, since it was an incredible piece of land, but still, this was the Big Island. People don't spend millions of dollars on property here, and certainly not on property up mauka, toward the mountain and hours away from a decent beach.) So we all just treated it as a sort of sanctuary. There were unofficial hiking trails winding through and areas set up where the local bird-watchers' society could spy for ʻapapane, the red honeycreeper with a song so varied and lovely it inspired dozens of legends of forest spirits; for ʻio, the endangered Hawaiian hawk, with its piercing cry; and the many, many other birds whose voices fill the silence of the forest. When I was a kid, I built forts back in there. (My mom pretended she didn't know about this habitual trespassing, since it was private property and all.)

I couldn't believe what I was hearing. "It sold?"

He nodded. "To a developer. Apparently, they're going to put in some kind of high-end spa, make it a destination, like Canyon Ranch in Arizona or Aro Ha in New Zealand. They're planning to drill down, hoping to reach some steam vents for a 'natural' sauna, open up some lava tubes for their visitors to explore, all of that."

"But that's crazy!" Mom said. "They can't know what the impact of that will be. Drilling?"

"They'll have to get someone on-site to make sure they don't set off an eruption or anything, but I bet it'll be somebody who doesn't know anything about Kīlauea or how our volcano will respond. It's crazy," my dad said.

"How can they give permits for something like that?" I asked. "It'll change the nature of the entire town! How many tourists are we talking?"

"Hundreds," Dad said. "More when the volcano is going off."

We are silent for a moment, imagining even *more* people, even *more* traffic clogged with tourist jeeps and convertibles. More crowds of people to fight through to be able to go on a hike in the national park, more rubbish left on the sides of the roads, more land being owned as vacation property and not someone's home.

"Well," Mom said brightly. "That would bring in so much work and money for the community. That's definitely a good thing." Mom could be a little Pollyanna sometimes. There's literally nothing she couldn't find a bright side of.

Dad shrugged. "That's true."

And I knew that it was. Our little town existed mostly because of tourists going to the national park down the road, and sometimes it felt like half the people in town ran a bed-and-breakfast or an Airbnb. We needed tourists to survive, just like everyone else in Hawai'i. And just like everyone else, we resented it.

It was hard not to feel like you were fighting for space in your own home when you had to get permission slips from hotels to be able to drive to a nearby beach, the hotels restricting access to land that was not theirs. It was hard not to feel angry when you couldn't get into another beach because the parking lot was full of rental cars. And it was definitely hard not to be enraged when you watched your 'āina being destroyed for yet another tourist attraction.

I didn't hate individual tourists. When I helped out in my uncle's store, they were always really nice and that was great. It was just the damage caused by the industry itself.

CHAPTER THREE

I SLEPT LATE THE NEXT MORNING. IT WAS SUMMER and I was a teenager, so it should be a given that I slept late, but my mom normally cranked the radio by nine a.m., so that the sounds of Hawaii Public Radio pontificating would force me to get moving. That didn't happen, and when I rolled over and saw that it was ten thirty, instead of thanking my lucky stars, I wondered what was wrong.

I found my mom in the bathroom scrubbing away at the tiles she had laid the day before.

"This was perfect, I swear," Mom said tightly. "I don't know what could have happened."

I tilted my head as I eyed the new tiles. They were definitely crooked. Like, *really* crooked, not like some small, unnoticeable thing that my mom might have done by accident.

"Do you need help?" I asked. "What could have happened?"

"I don't know!" Mom snapped. "Just . . . go finish up in the garage like I asked you to."

I drew back, affronted. "I finished the garage yesterday."

Mom turned around and gave me a look. "Really? That's what you call finished?"

I was about to argue, but she seemed so certain that I suddenly wasn't sure. I remembered delivering all the donations in the car—hard to forget that experience—and I *thought* I'd tidied everything up before I went, but maybe I'd missed something?

I grabbed a banana for breakfast and headed out to the garage, and . . . yeah. It was a mess. My dad's tools, some of them rusting and many of them unidentifiable, were piled on what we generously called his workbench but was really an old desk. Snorkels and fins, many of them so salt-crusted the rubber had begun to decay, were scattered in one corner, while a bucket of old tennis balls had fallen over, scattering them across the cement floor, which was strewn with dust and leaves that had accumulated over the years. I could have sworn I'd cleaned it all up, but I guess not. No wonder my mom was annoyed with me.

When Mom came to offer me lunch, I tried to look busy and self-sacrificing so she wouldn't be too mad at me for bailing on it yesterday.

"Take a break," she said. "My brother needs you at the store anyway."

"Oh no," I protested. "I can finish."

My mom rolled her eyes. "I know you'd rather be at the store. Go on. But you have to take your bike—I don't have time to drive you."

Tempting as it was to point out that I could drive myself, having successfully (as far as my mom knew) done so yesterday, I didn't waste another second arguing. I loved working at my uncle's store, and even if I didn't, anything was better than being in the garage. It was drizzling, but nothing that could really be called rain, so I pedaled steadily through the village until I reached the store on Old Volcano Road. I pulled my bike around the back like usual, chaining it to a thick bamboo tree.

The store was small, with every available square foot in use. The shelves were packed so closely together that it was hard for two people to squeeze past each other, but somehow it didn't feel claustrophobic. Everything but the wood floor was painted a bright, crisp white, so that the silvers and bronzes of the hardware section stood out. Uncle Danny waved as I took up my position behind the register, helping myself to a Spam musubi and a Rockstar as I went.

"That the last one?" he asked.

"Yeah. Ikaika says you should make more," I said as I peeled open the plastic wrap.

"If Ikaika Auna wants to spend an hour frying Spam first thing in the morning, he's welcome to come help."

I grinned. "Fair enough. Speaking of help, what do you need?"

"Can you do emergency rice? We're running low."

Here is what my uncle meant by emergency rice: we take the big bag of white rice he bought at the grocery store in Hilo and pour two cups' worth into smaller Ziploc bags and sell them at a serious markup. Highway robbery? Probably. But when you run out of rice and dinner is in an hour and the grocery store is forty-five minutes away, you buy the Ziploc bag.

    I measured rice and updated my uncle on the morning's mysteries.

    "That's weird," he said, frowning. "Your mom's great at tile work. She wouldn't have done it crooked."

    "Exactly!" I said. "And I'm telling you, I cleaned that garage yesterday."

    "Maybe it was the menehune," my uncle teased.

    I rolled my eyes. "Okay, sure, Uncle."

    "Could be, you know . . ." He came over and squeezed my shoulder. "You got this covered? I need to do inventory in the back."

    "Yeah, no worries!"

    As I continued measuring rice, my eye caught on a souvenir—a key chain with a smiling, chubby menehune with a round belly and a big grin and a shaka. It was awful. This kind of menehune are to the menehune from legends what the Lucky Charms leprechaun is to leprechauns of traditional lore. Which is to say, incredibly wrong and kind of racist. Like leprechauns, menehune were said to be helpful and incredibly skilled, smaller than humans and capable of disappearing into the forest. For instance, according to one story, Moʻokini Heiau on the other side of the island was built by menehune. We hiked there once to look around, but it was years ago and mostly all I remember was that it was a crazy hot day and too rocky to go swimming. The heiau was enormous and complex, with several different platforms and incredibly high walls. Not something that could have been done by a hapless gnome with a beer belly, which is what this key chain and other images like it would have you believe the menehune were.

There was a family legend on my dad's side, the side of my family that's part Hawaiian, that said we descended from the menehune. Who knew if it was true? It probably wasn't, and there probably were never menehune to begin with. But I still moved that ugly-ass key chain to the back of the rack, where I didn't have to see it.

The bells over the door rang, and I plastered on my best "customer smile." "Hi! Let me know if you need help finding anything."

The couple that walked in wore what I liked to call Hiker Tourist Chic. We're talking lots of REI, hiking boots that had barely been used, sun hats with neck protection, and Fitbits. Bonus points for fancy DSLR cameras.

"Do you have any kombucha?" the woman asked. "I feel so dehydrated—the sun is fierce out on the lava fields!"

"Yep!" I replied. "We have some local Big Island Booch in the case right back over there."

I heard the man say, "Oooh, some local IPA, too, that's cool," to which she snapped, "No! You need to hydrate!"

They brought their kombucha and energy bars up to the counter, and as I started ringing them up, the man asked, "Where can we go to see the lava flowing?"

"Oh, if you go in the evening, you can see a red glow down in Kīlauea crater...."

"Yeah, we saw that last night, but I mean, like, flowing. Doesn't it go on roads and stuff, so you can go right up to it?"

I blinked at him. "I mean . . . I guess, sometimes. It did flow into some neighborhoods, but, like, it's *really hot*, and you don't actually want to go right up to it. It being, you know, lava and all."

"Right! It's flowing into some neighborhoods. Remember we read that on the news, honey?"

The woman nodded absently, scrolling through her phone, so the man turned to me for confirmation.

"Um. Yeah, it did flow into some neighborhoods a couple of years ago. It was actually, uh, pretty devastating? A lot of people in Leilani Estates lost their homes."

The man quickly shifted to looking concerned. "Oh, wow. That's terrible. And I bet insurance doesn't cover acts of lava, huh?"

"Yeah, not really," I said.

"Well," he said, grinning awkwardly. "Guess we'll have to skip that experience this trip. What about some of the local cultural sites?"

"If you're interested in Hawaiian culture, you could go see some heiau. They're temples built by the ancient Hawaiians—"

The bells chimed again, and this time it was my auntie Paula, Uncle Danny's wife. "Emma! Hi!" She came around behind the counter to give me a kiss and took over ringing up the couple, which was absolutely fine with me. I went back to my rice measuring and listened to her give them her usual speech about the most picturesque places to go—'Akaka Falls, Waipi'o Valley Lookout, the botanical gardens, etc.

When the man asked about the heiau I'd mentioned, she said, "Oh yes, you could do that, but a lot of the time they're in the sun and you can get really hot." She laughed. "Anyway, Emma, when's the last time you went to a heiau?"

I frowned. "Um. A school field trip in the third grade?"

"Yeah, and I bet you had your head in a book the whole time!" She handed the man his change. "My niece, she's so different from the other kids here. Always reading and always watching, you know, those PBS costume dramas? You'd never know she was from Hawai'i!"

Something inside me squirmed, uncomfortable, but I squashed it back down. None of what she'd said was untrue, after all. I pasted a smile on my face and said, "According to C. S. Lewis, 'You can never get a cup of tea large enough or a book long enough,' and I completely agree with him."

The couple left with their mango kombuchas, and Auntie Paula and I finished up the emergency rice together, chatting about movies and TV shows and nothing at all.

After the rice, I helped my uncle restock and dusted off the small collection of local books and artwork he still carried even though hardly anybody ever bought them. To be honest, it probably didn't need to be done, but I was dragging out my time at the store as much as I could. All that was waiting for me at home was another month of cleanup and wedding prep. But my uncle knew this very well and sent me off with a "Tell my sister I said thanks for letting me borrow you" and another Rockstar to keep up my energy.

To put it all off for just a little while longer, I biked up Wright Road to the property that had just sold, the one that was destined to become some sort of spa. I wanted to see it again, to say goodbye to it, I guess, before it all changed. I knew they were going to need to clear some of the forest, but nothing could've prepared me for what I saw.

It was gone. Not all twenty-five acres, not yet, but the big ʻōhiʻa tree that I'd climbed and gotten stuck in and needed to be rescued from, and the fallen log that had served as the roof of the fort I made when I was ten, and the clump of tī that we picked leaves from and used to make lei for our school concert, twining the strands with our fingers while gripping the knotted leaves with our toes . . . they were all gone. In their place was a field of brown mud and broken branches, rocks and leaves churned together, tree roots exposed and shredded, like the remains of a battlefield.

I watched as a bulldozer moved back and forth, pushing fallen ʻōhiʻa trees and crushing the huge fronds of hāpuʻu ferns. Various workers, including architects and landscape designers, I guess, stood around, comparing charts and plans and whatever else.

I felt tears begin to prick. It wasn't just that I was watching my memories, my childhood, being destroyed. It was more than that. There was something about *this place*, about this forest, that felt in some ways like the last remaining piece of wildness left around here. What would it mean when it was gone?

This forest was more than just trees and rocks and moss. It was sacred. Which meant this was a desecration.

Swallowing the lump in my throat, I hauled my bike around and started pedaling home. But I didn't get far. The tears came in spite of myself, so I pulled over onto the grass on the side of the road, laid my bike on its side, and sat down, my head in my hands. I was shuddering, sobbing, crying harder than I could explain or even understood. They were just *trees*, after all. But it felt like so much more than that.

When at last I started to calm down, my eyes caught on something. There was a trail leading into the woods on the side of the road. This was not uncommon—wild pigs made trails all over the island—but this trail was bigger. I pushed up onto my knees, peering into the shadows, and I spotted something that looked like a lean-to. It resembled the fort I had made not so long ago. Was someone living back in there? Hawai'i struggled to house the homeless—it was a constant issue—but they mostly lived down the hill, where it was warmer. At an elevation of 3,800 feet, we lived in a cloud forest where it rained 255 days of the year, and even in the summer, overnight temperatures went down to the fifties.

The back of my neck prickled, sending a jolt down to the base of my spine. There was a sound, followed by some kind of movement behind the lean-to. I jumped to my feet, my heart thudding and my fingertips tingling with adrenaline. I hauled my bike back up and pedaled away as fast as I could.

CHAPTER FOUR

DESPITE ALL MY COMPLAINING ABOUT the work involved, I was excited about my sister's wedding. Being eleven years apart—hello, surprise baby here—we'd never squabbled like regular siblings and instead simply enjoyed the inevitable camaraderie that comes with having the same parents. When she left for college, I was shocked by the hole her departure left in my life. I was so used to going to her basketball games (even if I usually read through them) and having her friends around and having her art scattered all over. I missed her. And now Puʻulena was getting married, and I really liked Naomi, and I was going to be a bridesmaid, and that was all great—except it meant she would never live at home again. Which, obviously, I already knew would never happen, but I hadn't really felt it until now. Puʻulena and Naomi would buy a house and have a kid and live on the mainland to be close to Naomi's family. Besides, that's where Puʻulena's work was, and that was that.

I understood. After all, I knew that I was going to leave the islands someday, too. I wanted to go to college on the mainland, to live in a place where it snowed and I could be surrounded by people who liked the same things I liked—people who didn't think reading so much was weird and who liked music that wasn't necessarily either a) Hawaiian, or b) from ten to fifteen years ago. Hozier was just now getting radio play here.

The knock on my door interrupted my moping and "All Things End" listening. My mom stuck her head in. "Did you feed Mālie?" she asked.

"Not since this morning," I said. "I'm only supposed to do it in the mornings."

My mom rolled her eyes. "Yes, Emma. I just wondered if maybe you'd happened, out of the kindness of your heart, to feed her dinner, because she didn't come when I shook her dish."

My heart sank. Mālie was one of those dogs who behaved like she was perpetually starving, even though we fed her exactly as much as we were supposed to for a dog of her size. If she heard the sound of food, she came running. And if she hadn't, then that meant—

"She got out *again*?" I moaned.

My mom sighed. "I guess so. I'll go drive around looking for her."

I scrambled to my feet. "I'll come."

"Let's split up," Mom said. "We'll cover more ground that way. Take your bike and ride around the neighborhood—maybe she didn't get far. I'll drive to Snookie's house."

I hunted through the pile of laundry on my floor for a pair of clean socks. I shoved my feet into my battered once-pink-but-now-muddy-brown Converse and tucked the laces in—no time to tie them. We had to find Mālie, and fast, because if she got hit by a car, she wouldn't walk away from it.

It wasn't dark yet, but it would be soon—even in the summer it didn't stay light later than seven thirty. If she hadn't gone to Snookie's, Mālie might have gone up to the property at the back of Wright Road—sometimes she and I would explore that jungle together, and I knew it was a place she found familiar and welcoming.

Sure enough, as I rounded the corner onto Wright Road, I saw her in the distance, running uphill.

"Mālie!" I yelled. "Stay!"

She ignored me. I heard the clicking of nails on the road and turned to see Snookie running after me. He passed me, the little jerk, and went chasing after Mālie.

I panted, struggling to keep up. When I crested the hill, I was able to pick up speed, gaining on the dogs. I let out a groan of frustration as they vanished into the bushes about twenty feet ahead of me. I skidded to a stop and left my bike on its side next to the road.

"Goddamn it," I yelled. "Mālie! Get back here!" I ran after them, but then hesitated at the forest's edge.

Snookie and Mālie had run down the trail leading to the lean-to in the woods.

I did not want to go in there, not even a little bit. The sun hadn't set quite yet, but it was dark beneath the trees. I couldn't tell if whatever (or whomever) I'd heard back in the woods was still there, but I felt a twinge of discomfort on the back of my neck. The dogs weren't barking; they were just snuffling around making dog noises in the undergrowth, but I couldn't hear anything over them.

"Mālie!" I called. "Come!"

She didn't bother to respond. I took a deep breath, hunched my shoulders, and plunged into the darkness after them. They were sniffing around the lean-to, but thankfully there was no noise or movement coming from inside it. I crept up and grabbed Mālie by her collar. She turned and gave me a loving lick.

"Yeah, whatever," I told her. "You're still in trouble."

I clipped on her leash and turned to go, but . . . I stopped. I knew I should just head home, but despite how eerie the clearing was, curiosity had gotten the better of me. I ran a hand over the lean-to. The structure was formed under a large fallen tree, with sticks and hāpuʻu fronds serving as the walls and the roof. Tugging Mālie, I moved toward the entrance and peered inside.

My breath caught in my throat, and it was all I could do not to scream. There was a figure lying on the ground.

Oh, God. What if this is a dead body?

Gingerly, I kicked out a foot and prodded at it. It didn't move. I swallowed hard and kicked it again.

"That doesn't feel like a pet. You shouldn't kick your pets. No kicking."

I jumped back so fast, I fell onto my butt in the dirt and dead leaves. "I'm so sorry," I gasped. "I . . . I didn't mean to kick you. Are you okay? Do you need help?"

The boy—for it was a boy's voice—still didn't move but lay curled on his side, turned away from me. "Help," he said. "Help who? Help what?"

He sounded so lost—hopeless, even, as if he couldn't even conceive of the idea of someone wanting to help him. I reached out a hand and touched his shoulder. "Hey," I said gently. "It's okay. I can go get somebody, all right? Is there someone I can call?"

He rolled over so suddenly he startled me again, and I snatched my hand away. "Somebody. I'm not somebody."

I stared at him in the dim light and realized with a shock that I knew him. His face was filthy, and his gold-tipped hair was crusted with dirt, but I recognized him all the same. He was the boy from the skate park, the one from Hilo. "How did you get here?" I asked. "What's your name? Where do you live?"

What happened to you? I wondered to myself.

"I don't live," he said.

I sighed. Communication was clearly not his strong point. "All right, come on," I said. "You can come home with me, and we will figure this out." *Or my mom will*, I added silently.

I reached out my hand again to help him up, but he shuddered away. "No," he said. "Nonononononono."

"What do you mean, no?" I said, exasperated. "You can't stay here! It's getting dark! Your family must be terrified for you. We have to get you home."

I tugged at his shoulder, and he rolled away from me, scrabbling in the dirt. He pressed up against the wall of his lean-to, and it started to collapse. "My home," he moaned. "My home is breaking."

"*This* is not your home," I said. "You live in Hilo, remember? I almost hit you with my car? Any of this sound familiar?"

"Nononononono—"

"Okay, let's not start that again." I reached for my phone to call my mom, only to realize that in my rush to find Mālie, I'd left it behind in my room, probably still playing Mournful Indie Music. The dogs, sensing Hilo's distress, pushed past me into the lean-to, licking and sniffing at him and of course further destroying his pitiful shelter. I rubbed my forehead against the sudden tension headache and sighed. "Look, you can't stay here, okay? You need to come with me."

"NO!" Surging to his feet, Hilo knocked down the roof of his lean-to and ran out, running over me in the process. Snookie and Mālie started to chase after him, but I yanked on Mālie's leash, and Snookie wouldn't leave without her. I climbed to my feet and tried to follow . . . but he was gone.

CHAPTER FIVE

I DIDN'T TELL ANYONE I'D FOUND A LOST BOY IN the forest.

I should have, I know. Obviously, I know that. He clearly needed help, and his parents were likely looking for him, and *of course* the right thing to do would've been to make sure they found him. I should have told my mom immediately. She would have called the police, and they would have found him, and he would have been home by morning.

But I didn't, because honestly I couldn't be sure it had actually happened. How had he ended up there? It didn't make any sense, and I had to wonder if I hadn't just imagined the whole thing.

By the time I'd dragged Mālie home and gotten ahold of my mom to let her know she could stop looking, the whole experience no longer felt quite real. It didn't make any sense, after all—I had *just seen him* a few days before, and he'd been quite normal. I mean, it's not like I knew him well, but he had definitely not been in speaking-nonsense-and-living-in-the-dirt mode. The only evidence that he'd been there at all was a knocked-down lean-to that no longer looked like anything but a pile of sticks and ferns.

When I was younger, my imagination had often gotten the better of me. I'd have conversations with things in the woods—creatures, spirits, you name it—only, being a little kid, I didn't understand that they were pretend. Somehow, I genuinely thought they were really happening. I'd tell my parents or my friends about them, and they'd nod along. Looking back now, I realized they must've thought I was as delirious as the boy in the woods was.

And considering how weird everything was last night, I told myself I must have imagined the whole thing.

So instead of telling my mom about the boy in the forest, I decided to bring him food. If he didn't exist, well, then I'd have some snacks. I'd first noticed the lean-to days ago, so if he'd really been there that whole time, he must have been starving. In the morning, I made some sandwiches and filled up some bottles of water. After rushing my way through the day's wedding-related tasks, I biked back up to the woods where I'd seen him, knowing full well that I'd find no sign of him, because, clearly, he'd never existed in the first place. Except...

He was there. He was real.

He had rebuilt his shelter, sort of. The lean-to was a little bedraggled, the sticks not aligned as neatly as before, the moss carpet that had served as his bed torn up by the tender attentions of Snookie and Mālie. As I crept in closer, bearing my offering of lunch, I heard him talking to himself.

"Hilo?" I said softly.

He turned around, startled. When he saw it was me, he turned back. "You didn't say she was coming," he said.

I looked over, trying to see whom or what he might have been talking to, besides the trees. There was nothing, of course. I busied myself with unpacking the sandwiches, spreading open the waxed paper to serve as a kind of plate. "Here," I said. "You must be hungry. I hope you're not allergic to peanuts." I hadn't really thought about that.

Hilo glanced over and looked at the sandwich as if he didn't quite recognize what it was. "Hungry," he said thoughtfully. He turned back to the fallen log he'd been talking to. "Are you hungry?"

As I watched Hilo, something moved. Out of the corner of my eye, it looked almost like a figure, something or *someone* made out of the forest. I shook my head, ordering myself sternly to keep it together. One of us had to maintain their grip on reality.

"Fine, then," Hilo said. "But I can't eat that," he said, indicating a fuzzy handful of hāpuʻu pulu. "I tried already."

I pushed the sandwich at him, pressing it into his hand. "Look, just eat this, okay? You can argue with your imaginary friend later."

Hilo held it in his palm, squishing it slightly before finally taking a bite. And then he took another, and another, and the sandwich was gone in less than a minute.

"Here," I said. "Have some water."

Hilo looked at the water bottle as if he didn't quite know what it was, and then tipped it into his mouth. Half the water ran down his chest, soaking through his T-shirt, but at least he got something.

"Well, I'm sorry, but it's not raining right now, so I can't drink rainwater," he told the log.

"Actually, it is rainwater," I said. "We're on catchment. All our water comes from the sky."

Hilo cocked his head at me. "Not from the faucet?"

I sighed heavily. "Yes, it does come from the faucet. But we're not on county water out here in the boonies. We get it from a water tank, which collects water from the roof. So, you know, it is rainwater. If that's something that's important to you."

Hilo nodded sagely. "Ua. Rain. It is life. Or so he says."

I glanced over at the "person" he was talking to, but there was just a fallen log. As I looked back at Hilo, however, I could've sworn I caught a glimpse of something—someone—leaning against the log.

But when I looked back again, it was just a log. As, of course, it had always been.

I sat with Hilo as he ate another sandwich. He talked to me sometimes, but mostly he talked to the log, saying things like, "e kala mai iʻau," "lilo au," "'Ōlelo ka ulu lāʻau," and "hoʻololi kea o." I didn't speak Hawaiian and for some reason had assumed he didn't, either. And yet, there he was, talking fluently to himself in ʻŌlelo Hawaiʻi.

"Who are you talking to?" I asked him.

Hilo turned and gave me a disapproving look, like I'd interrupted an important conversation. *"Him,"* he said significantly, gesturing at the log.

"Who is he?"

"He didn't say." He cocked his head as if listening and then frowned at me. "You don't see him?"

I found myself looking at the log just to double-check that there really wasn't anyone there, even though of course there wasn't. "No?" I said uncertainly. And for an instant, I genuinely wasn't sure—because I saw it again, that suggestion of a person, small but sturdy.

But then I blinked, and it was gone.

Hilo shrugged and turned back to his discussion.

It was kind of a weird thing to notice right then, but I couldn't help it—despite the dirt and sweat, Hilo was kinda hot. It was like looking at a young Hawaiian warrior from centuries ago, only his jeans were torn and he had dead leaves in his hair. He didn't seem anything like the annoying skater/surfer punk I'd met at Cooper Center—it was like he'd been anointed by the gods, granted a kind of soulfulness that I wouldn't have thought he possessed.

Then again, maybe it had been there all along, underneath. This wasn't the sort of thing I ought to have been paying attention to right then, but the truth was I couldn't take my eyes off him.

As he ate and spoke words I couldn't understand to a person who wasn't there, I thought about those times in my life that I had seen, or thought I'd seen, something that wasn't there. Like those imaginary conversations I'd told my friends and family about. But that was the thing—what I thought was real at the time was simply my brain misinterpreting my surroundings.

It's like when you're walking along the street and not really paying attention and it looks like there is a dog or something on the side of the road up ahead, only it can't be a dog because its neck is way too long or it's too tall or the wrong shape, and then you look more closely and your brain adjusts and you realize it was just a clump of bushes the whole time.

But what if it *wasn't* a clump of bushes? What if the first thing you saw was right and your brain just couldn't handle it? What if the bush was the misinterpretation, and the elongated dog was real?

The more I thought about it, the more my memories came flooding back. But could I trust them? I remembered playing with the dog, with its snaking neck and long, stick-like legs. I remembered stroking its rough, bark-like fur. I remembered watching it scamper up a tree and wishing I could follow.

I remembered the leaf that was a lizard but wasn't, and how that tiny moʻo crawled up my arm and nestled in my hair and stayed there all afternoon while I played in the forest, until my mom removed the leaf at the end of the day and told me it was time to get into the bath.

I remembered the ʻio that soared over the woods behind my house, its plaintive screech guiding me to a little clearing, the mossy floor somehow free of uluhe or ginger, where I could lie back and watch the hawk and its mate dancing above me in the blue sky, while tiny droplets of water beaded together on the moss and moved in their own small hula below.

I also remembered the last time I ever saw something like that.

I'd always told my parents and my sister about the things I saw, and they always treated my stories as if they were real because they saw how real they were to me. But one day, when I was ten, I came running into the house, eager to show off the new friend I had made. I cupped the beetle in my hands, its black iridescence sparkling with an indigo-and-copper rainbow, and giggled as I felt it skittering around and tasting the salt on my palms.

Carefully I opened my hands to show my mom and dad, and they dutifully oohed and aahed. But then someone I hadn't even noticed, a neighbor who had dropped by for a visit, peered in as well. "But that's a lava rock," they said. "A pretty, shiny one. But not a beetle."

My mom explained that I had a powerful imagination. "Emma is such a fanciful wild child—she's always imagining her creatures and telling us her little stories about them. It's so sweet, isn't it?"

"Oh," the neighbor said doubtfully. "Well, it's nice that she's so dreamy, I guess. But you might want to make sure she can tell what's real and what isn't. You wouldn't want her telling stories or fibs to the other kids."

I looked at my parents and realized that they saw a rock and had never seen the beetle—when they admired the creatures I showed them, they had been the ones who were pretending.

I looked down at my cupped hands, and just like that, the beetle was no longer there. I saw a rock, too, and I understood that it had always been a rock. From then on, I saw the bushes and not the dog. The moʻo stayed a leaf, and the hawks no longer called to me.

When he'd finished eating, Hilo squatted in the dirt, muttering to himself. "I'm not me, I'm not me, ʻaʻole au au, I'm not me." He peered at me, his eyes unfocused. "Make me me, girl."

"I . . . I don't know how," I stammered.

In one swift motion, Hilo stood up and charged off into the forest. I scrambled to my feet and shoved the balls of crumpled waxed paper into my pockets before rushing after him. "Where are you going?" I called.

He didn't answer. He just ran, dodging through ferns and jumping over roots and fallen trees. He moved with so much ease, it was as though the branches were parting to let him pass. This was not my experience of running through the woods. I got scratched by uluhe twigs that seemed to jut out right at eye level. I tripped over fallen hāpuʻu and got my feet tangled by ʻieʻie vines. I sank in mud up to my ankles and slipped, twisting my ankle. It was as if the forest was trying to make it as difficult as possible for me to make my way through. As I pushed myself to my feet, I saw—or thought I saw—a shadow move, and the vine I'd tripped over straightened back upright. I watched as the shadow wavered, solidifying into a short, stocky figure.

"Come, girl!" Hilo shouted, and the shadow vanished.

"What the hell?" I gasped, and ran on. I was so freaked out that when Hilo stopped suddenly in front of me, I almost crashed into him.

"Why," I panted, "are we running?"

Hilo ignored me, which I'd pretty much expected. He laid his palm flat on the trunk of a giant ʻōhiʻa tree, his hand tanned against the craggy gray bark.

"I'm sorry," he said softly. He closed his eyes and bowed his head.

I felt a sudden impulse to reach out to him, comforting him in some way, but before I knew it, he was off and running again. I chased him from tree to tree, and each time we stopped he apologized.

Finally, I couldn't take it anymore, or my lungs couldn't, anyway. I grabbed him by the shoulders and spun him around to face me, gripping him tightly. He was a lot stronger than I was and could have kept running if he'd really wanted to, but he didn't. He stopped and focused on me, at least for the moment.

"Hilo. What are you sorry for? What did you do?"

He stared at me. And then he took off running again.

My shoulders slumped. What was I doing? This was ridiculous. I should go home. I should get some help. I should definitely not be running through the woods chasing a boy who seemed almost possessed.

But almost immediately, Hilo stopped again and turned to look at me. When I didn't follow him, he walked back over to where I was standing and took my hand in his. He didn't say anything, but he pulled me after him at a more reasonable pace, and the branches seemed to move for me, too.

It wasn't long before I began to hear shouting. I'd completely lost my sense of direction during our haphazard apology run through the woods, but when we came upon the devastation of churned dirt and fallen trees, I knew we had reached the construction site.

Hilo squeezed my hand, and I turned to look at him.

"I know," I said gently. "I hate it, too."

They'd cleared a bit more land since the last time I'd been here, but not as much as I would have expected—and as Hilo and I stood watching from the edge of the forest, unseen, it was soon clear why.

"I want to know who is responsible for this!" The man shouting was in jeans and a work shirt, like everyone else on-site, but he clearly wasn't just any worker—there wasn't a speck of dirt on him.

Squatting, he pulled at a rock jammed into the sprocket between the links that allowed the bulldozer to run on its track like a tank. He pulled and pulled, but the rock was stuck fast.

It was clear the bulldozer was going nowhere.

The man marched over to another, larger bulldozer, and while I couldn't make out his yelling, it was clear that bulldozer wasn't working, either.

The yelling went on for some time, while the workers stood around, shifting their weight and looking uncomfortable. Finally, Mr. Clean Jeans seemed to run out of steam. He walked back over to the workers, where we could hear him again.

"This gets fixed. I don't care how. I want it fixed *today*. Those machines are back up and running by tomorrow, you hear me? Or so help me, you're all fired."

Whoever was shoving those rocks into the bulldozers was a goddamn hero, as far as I was concerned.

I pulled Hilo out of there before anyone spotted us.

By the time we got back to his campsite, it had been hours. My parents would be wondering where I was. Hilo squatted before his leafy bed, and my heart twisted. What was I doing? I couldn't leave him here, not now that I knew for sure that he was real. It was one thing to spend a few hours running around the woods, but it was another to purposely leave someone alone in the woods, with no shelter and no food.

I needed to go home and get my mom.

"Hilo," I said softly. "I have to go, but I'll be back, okay? I'm going to get some help. You'll be all right soon. I promise."

Hilo's shoulders hunched over, and he wouldn't look at me. I sighed and turned to head back to the road when his arm shot out, grabbing me by the ankle. "Don't tell," he whispered. "Please. I have to fix it."

I shut my eyes tightly. I *should* tell someone. I knew I should. He could get sick, or hurt, or lost, and I wouldn't be able to find him again, and then I would be responsible.

And I understood, right then, the real reason why I was considering not telling my mother about Hilo. It wasn't that I hadn't been sure he was really there. It was because, if I did, she would call the police, and his parents would come get him, and then he would go back to seeing logs and bushes instead of whatever imagined, impossible things he was seeing now. And I would never have the chance to see anything like that ever again. Hilo was opening the door between worlds that I had slammed shut years ago. I didn't know how to open it again without him.

Did this make me a terrible person? I mean, it wasn't that great to let a kid stay lost in the woods, clearly unwell, just so I could, what? Explore my third eye? Imaginary forest friends were fine when you were a kid, but eventually we all have to grow up. I knew that. And yet I wasn't quite ready to let go of the possibility that maybe, just maybe, the things I had seen were real. I'd lost the ability to connect with whatever Hilo saw, but what if I could get it back again?

I glanced sideways at Hilo; whispered, "I won't," and left him there.

CHAPTER SIX

WHEN I GOT HOME, I SAID A quick hello to my mom, who looked at me with wide eyes and asked that I please change clothes because goodness I was muddy; what on earth had I been doing? I mumbled something about falling off my bike and ran to take a quick shower. I wrapped my hair in a towel and pulled out my phone to call Ana.

Ana was my best friend, and she was the only person who'd ever really believed me about the things I saw. We'd met the very first day of kindergarten. Her dad was a lawyer, too, and so our parents knew one another and introduced us. We peered at each other from behind our parents' legs, and that was all it took. We were basically inseparable from then on. Kindergarten was the one and only time we were ever in a class together—after that, the school made sure to keep us separated, so that we would, you know, pay at least some attention in class.

Which was all well and good during the school year, because at least we could hang out at recess and after school, but in the summer, it was really hard to get together, because, unfortunately, Ana lived over ninety minutes away. Our parents commuted into Hilo—mine from Volcano, hers from Ninole—so while Hilo was an acceptable place to get together, going over to each other's houses was a challenge.

Which was a bummer because she loved my house and I loved hers. I may have had mist and forests, but Ana had hammocks and a nearby waterfall we could go swimming beneath.

I wished desperately that she were here right now. Ana would know what to do because Ana always knew what to do. I did well in school, but Ana was a straight-A student who was in all the clubs and won all the awards. Seriously, if there was an award available, in any subject, it was Ana's. Most Likely to Succeed? Our class voted for Ana, every time. I'd be lying if I said this didn't make it hard to be friends with her sometimes because, of course, I would have liked it if *just once* I won something. I'd never even gotten the higher score on a single test.

But Ana never bragged about it or said anything to make me feel bad—it was just the way it was. She worked really hard in school, much harder than I did. And added to that, she was just really, really smart.

I could definitely use some of those smarts right now.

Ana's forehead filled the screen. She was bent over her guitar, working out what sounded to me like a very complicated chord progression. "Hi, Em, what's up?" she asked.

"Are you anywhere your parents can hear you?" I asked quietly.

She looked up at me then. "Um, yeah? Why?"

I made a face at her. Obviously, I couldn't explain why right at that moment.

She cleared her throat. "Hey, Mom, I'm going to finish practicing later, okay? I'm just going to go, uh, feed the chickens."

I heard Ana's mom say something, presumably in the affirmative, because Ana started moving outside. There wasn't much in the way of cell service out where Ana lived, and there was no way she could make it all the way out to the chicken coop and still get Wi-Fi from the house. She ended up crouching in her garage, one that rivaled mine for clutter—or at least, my pre-wedding prep garage, anyway.

"What's going on?"

I told Ana everything, right from the beginning. I told her about meeting Hilo at Cooper Center and then finding him in the woods a couple of days later. I told her about the development going up on Wright Road, and she moaned in sympathy. She was the one who had helped me build that fort back in there, so long ago. I told her how Hilo seemed to see things that weren't there and hear them and talk to them, the way I used to be able to do. I told her that I felt like I was on the cusp of being able to see them, too. "Ugh,"

I moaned. "It's too much to handle on my own. Can't you come over this weekend?"

Ana shook her head. "I really wish I could. I asked my dad about it just this morning, but they have to work all week and next weekend is banana harvest."

Ana's parents had a small banana farm, and she always had to help pick when they were ripe. I'd done it, and it sucked. I made a face in sympathy. "So what do I do?" I asked.

Ana gave me a look. "Emma. You tell someone where he is."

I should have known she was going to say that. Ana tended to be a little more practical than I was.

"Yeah, I can't do that. First of all, he asked me not to. And before you say he doesn't get to decide, just listen. I think whatever he sees is really there, Ana."

She sighed. "Emma, I get it. You experienced something magical, something inexplicable and meaningful when we were kids. Of course, you don't want to let that go. But this guy is lost in the woods, and however it is that he can see them—and I believe you that he can—something is clearly very wrong, and he needs help."

"I can help him," I said in a small voice.

Ana rolled her eyes. "I'm talking more help than a couple of sandwiches, Emma. He needs to go home."

"Look, I can't explain why, but it feels important to keep all of this a secret. I don't know what they are, the things he can see. Maybe they're forest spirits, who knows, but they're *real.* I know now that I didn't make them up when I was little, because *he sees them, too.* But if I tell someone, they'll take him out of the woods and that will be that. I'll never know what they are."

Ana had her thinking face on, her heavy eyebrows furrowed, and my heart lifted a little because it meant she was coming up with a plan.

"Okay," she said at last. "What are the risks involved? He could freeze to death, or at the very least get really sick, and he could starve. Like, that could actually happen if he's as out of it as you say he is. So first things first, you need to get him food, water, and warmth."

I nodded quickly. "I can do that."

"And." She looked at me sternly. "This can't go on for too long. I hear what you're saying, and I understand why you don't want to tell anyone yet. But this is actually dangerous—and, like, *he* might be dangerous—so you can't drag this out forever."

This was definitely true. "Five days," I said. "At the end of five days, I'll tell someone. I promise."

Ana looked up, and I could hear her mom hollering in the background. "Okay, be right up!" She looked back at me. "I've got to go. Report back on how it goes?"

"I will. Thanks for, you know, listening. And believing me."

Ana smiled at me. "Always."

I had meant to go back to visit Hilo in the morning, with breakfast, more water, and a sleeping bag, but the day's wedding tasks were piling up. Literally.

My mom dumped four bags filled with tiny lauhala boxes onto the dining room table.

"Um. What's all of that?"

"Favors," Mom said shortly.

I scrunched up my nose. "Favors? I thought Puʻulena wanted a low-key wedding."

"And these are low-key favors," my mom answered. "We're not doing anything fancy; we're just drying some flowers and ferns and adding some sea glass and some chocolate-covered macadamia nuts. And then we're putting them in these boxes and tying them with raffia."

"Right," I said, nodding. "So we're filling and tying boxes today?"

"No, we still need the flowers and ferns and sea glass. I'll get the macadamia nuts closer to the wedding day. Today, I need you to collect flowers and ferns so we can dry them out in time."

"Can't we just, I don't know, buy some dried flowers?"

My mom just stared at me, and I sighed. "Right, obviously not, because this is a DIY wedding. What kinds of flowers am I picking, lehua?"

"No! We can't pick the lehua; the ʻōhiʻa tree is in danger enough as it is. Just pick hydrangea. My brother said you can pick from his bushes."

"Wait, how come I have to go over to Uncle Danny's? We have tons of hydrangea here."

"We can't pick from *here*," Mom said, exasperated. "The wedding is going to be here. We need the flowers to stay on the bushes here so it looks pretty. And I'll need you to bike over there and back. I can't drive you. And before you ask, I'm not going to let you take the car again until you have your license. I don't know what I was thinking. What if you'd gotten into an accident?"

I elected not to argue that point, given how close I'd come to doing precisely that. Even so, this task seemed a bit, well, impossible. "Mom, how am I going to haul several bushes' worth of hydrangea over here on a *bike*?"

"Emma, please, just figure it out, okay? I have so much to do today. If it rains, the pond is going to flood the wedding site, and we have to level the ground where the tent is going to go, and get the lights hung, and—"

"Okay, no problem," I said quickly. I could hear that Mom was shifting into panic mode, and that wasn't good for anybody. "I'll handle it; don't worry."

Which was how I found myself biking over to my uncle's house with a big black garbage bag. I figured I could haul it over my shoulder and try to keep from jostling the flowers too much. He and Auntie Paula were at the store, so I pulled out my clippers and started cutting away. The hydrangea were big and fat, like puffballs of powder-blue blossoms, and their sharp green scent filled the air. It didn't take long to fill the garbage bag, and soon enough it was slung over my shoulder as I pedaled.

But, um, it turned out that a garbage bag filled with poking stems and fragile flowers was not actually all that easy to bike with. I made it about fifty feet before giving up, leaving my bike against the side of my uncle's house, and walking home with the bag in hand.

I kept my head down as I trudged and fantasized about the guilt trip I was going to pull on Mom for making me do this.

When Hilo spoke behind me, I screamed and dropped the garbage bag.

"You've been following me from the front," he said.

I put a hand over my chest, trying to get my heart rate back to normal. "That is not a thing," I said. "*You* are following *me*."

Hilo frowned at me and looked down at the garbage bag. "Why?" he asked.

I shrugged. "It's something I have to do for my sister's wedding," I said.

Hilo nodded like that made perfect sense. He picked up the garbage bag and slung it over his shoulder. "Keep following me," he said, gesturing for me to lead the way.

I hesitated. I wasn't exactly sure I wanted him to know where I lived, seeing as how he was a tad unpredictable and—possibly—dangerous. On the other hand, I was very sure I didn't want to haul all that hydrangea by myself. We walked together down the road, and Hilo never complained, though I'm sure the stems must have been stabbing him just as painfully as they'd been poking me.

Occasionally a car would pass us, and I would give a wave and get a wave back, but no one stopped. Whoever Hilo was, no one recognized him.

We stopped outside my house, at the end of my driveway, and I took the bag of flowers back from Hilo. "Thanks," I said awkwardly. "If you wait a minute, I can go get you some food."

Hilo smiled, his eyes crinkling at the edges, and a tiny dimple appeared beside his mouth. My heart did a little flip, and this time it wasn't because I'd been startled. "I like peanut butter," he said cheerfully.

"Right," I said. "Okay, I'll be back in a minute."

Hilo sat down cross-legged on the side of the road. The grass was still wet from the rain that had fallen the night before, but he looked comfortable enough.

My mom was busy out by the pond, and I made it into the house without being seen. I grabbed an old sleeping bag from the back of my closet, filled some water bottles, made the sandwiches as quickly as possible, and brought everything back to Hilo. With a resigned sigh, I sat down next to him on the grass. Wet butts in Hawai'i were pretty much a constant state of affairs. I handed him a sandwich and placed a bottle of water between us. We ate without talking, but it wasn't an awkward kind of silence. Or at least, it wasn't any more awkward than eating lunch with a boy who couldn't even tell me his own name should have been.

We sat in the shade of a tall and thin ʻōlapa tree, listening to its fluttering leaves as it swayed, the hula dancer of the forest. One of its leaves floated down beside me, and I ripped into it with my fingernails, releasing its sweet mango scent. The small black berries provided food for the croaking ʻōmaʻo and the ʻalalā, the Hawaiian crow. I always hoped that somehow I would see an ʻalalā come pecking at the ʻōlapa berries, squawking its dominance. I loved crows for their otherworldly spookiness and also for their raucous joy—for their ability to be entirely *themselves*, without care for what anyone else might think.

Beneath the ʻōlapa grew naupaka kuahiwi, the naupaka of the mountains, a bush made of spiky leaves and delicate white half flowers, the petals forming a semicircle, as if the other half of the blossom had been torn off.

"Do you know the moʻolelo of the naupaka?" I asked. "Of course you do," I answered myself, when Hilo only blinked at me. "Everyone knows some version of it." I drew a breath to summon up the ability to tell the story the way I'd been told, again and again.

"Naupaka was a princess; an aliʻi beloved by everyone who knew her—but particularly by Kaui, a handsome fisherman who often saw her walking along the beach. The very first time their eyes met, they knew they belonged together. He placed a small white flower in her hair as proof of his love.

"But Kaui was makaʻāinana, a commoner, and when Naupaka sought guidance from the elders of her village, the kupuna shook their heads in sadness. 'We cannot sanction this marriage,' they said. 'It is forbidden.'

"But Kaui and Naupaka did not give up. They walked for three days and three nights, climbing from the shore to the mountaintop, crossing rivers and valleys and all the changing landscape of the island as they went, in search of a high priest who might be able to help them. When at last they found the Kahuna Nui, he gazed upon them with sorrow. 'I see the strength of your love,' he said. 'But I cannot grant your request to marry—that power can come only from the gods.'

"And so Kaui and Naupaka raised their faces to the heavens in prayer—but the sun did not shine on them. The storm clouds gathered, and rain began to fall with the gods' regret as they refused. Naupaka bent her head in grief. She removed the flower Kaui had given her from her hair and tore it in half. 'I will stay here in the mountains,' she said. 'And you must go back to the ocean. We cannot be together.'

"And so today there are two varieties of the naupaka blossom—the naupaka kuahiwi and the naupaka kahakai. Each blooms in perfect half flowers, belonging together, but always apart."

When I'd finished, Hilo reached out and picked a flower, handing it to me. "Sad," he said.

"Sad," I agreed. "And kind of a weird story for me to tell, I guess," I added with a grimace, twirling the flower with my fingers so that, as it blurred with motion, it looked whole and complete.

Hilo shrugged. "Two worlds," he said. "Always separate now."

I had no idea what he meant and reached out to stop him from putting the blue-black naupaka berries into his mouth.

"Poison?" he asked.

"I don't think so," I said doubtfully. "But they don't taste good. Anyway, I should be getting back to work. Do you know your way, um, home?"

Hilo took a final swig of water and nodded. "They'll help me if I get lost," he said.

I flicked a glance into the bushes. I hadn't noticed any of the creatures, or spirits, or whatever they were, but that didn't mean they weren't there. "Okay," I said. "That's good, I guess."

Hilo grinned and got to his feet. "I will tell them you said hello." He slung the sleeping bag over his shoulder before he turned and began walking back up the road.

I didn't end up complaining to Mom about what a pain hauling the hydrangea had been. After all, it hadn't really been *my* pain, since Hilo had done all the work. But when she saw the giant bag and put together how awkward it must have been without my saying so, she felt really bad about it and promised to chill out about the wedding from then on.

"It's just, I do all this work and then it seems like it keeps getting undone! It's making me feel crazy!"

"I totally get it," I assured her. "It's fine; I promise. And we'll figure out how to get it done."

I wasn't sure how we would, exactly, because the truth was, she was right. I didn't know what was going on, but I knew she wasn't imagining things. Projects we'd completed and crossed off of The List were somehow incomplete by morning. The bathroom tiles, the garage, and now the lights had gone awry, too. While I'd been chasing after Hilo the day before, running from one 'ōhi'a tree to the next on Hilo's apology tour, Uncle Mike had come over to hang the outdoor lights for the wedding, just like he'd promised. And yet, there they were, neatly coiled in the corner of the garage, as if they'd never been touched.

It was enough to make anyone feel crazy. Maybe whatever had happened to Hilo was somehow catching.

In any case, to Mom's credit, that night we took a break. Dad picked up my bike on his way home and brought Thai takeout with him. Because of the influx of tourists, Volcano had three restaurants, way more than could be sustained by residents alone, *and* two food trucks—but one of the restaurants and both of the food trucks served only Thai food, so choices were pretty much a variety of Thai. There were loyalists in every camp, with people going exclusively to their preferred Thai option. We tended to get food from the restaurant because my sister and two of my cousins had worked there while they were in high school. Also because as far as we were concerned, it was the best of the bunch.

We played Scrabble over our massaman curry, and while Dad still won like always, I did manage to corner three of the triple-word-score squares, and Mom somehow got away with using the word *cinq* even though it's French.

After the game concluded, Mom and Dad went to watch television while I curled up on a chair with *Wuthering Heights*. I'd reached the final chapters, and, obviously, I needed to finish it as quickly as humanly possible, although of course I already knew how it ended. When at last I looked up, the house was dark. Mom and Dad had gone off to bed.

So it was pretty late when, yawning, I went out to the garage to deal with the hydrangeas. According to a cursory Google search, the best way to dry hydrangeas is to leave them in a hot car for a day, so all we had to do was send them to work with Dad. Trouble was, he needed to leave obscenely early because he had eight a.m. court that he hadn't fully prepped for. Rather than get up at dawn to spread out the flowers in the trunk, I had decided to do it before bed . . . only I'd lost track of time, and now it was past midnight.

I was tired and most of me was still somewhere on the Yorkshire moors, so at first, I didn't even notice. But then I saw, out of the corner of my eye, the glint of lights, twinkling like gold in the dark night. It was coming from the backyard, over by the pond where my mom had been working all day—right where we were planning on holding Puʻulena's wedding ceremony.

I didn't have a sweatshirt on, and the temperature had gone down with the sun, so I wrapped my arms across my chest to keep warm as I made my way through the yard to investigate. I was also wearing slippers (a.k.a. flip-flops, though no self-respecting person in Hawai'i would call them that), and my feet were getting wet and grassy. If this was all just my overactive imagination, I was going to be very annoyed at it.

When I reached the pond, I looked up at the trees, baffled and awestruck. Somehow the twinkle lights had been strung up in the trees, twined around the branches, sparkling as if they were in conversation with the stars overhead.

This was impossible. I had just seen these same lights in the garage this afternoon. Uncle Mike wouldn't have come over to do this in the middle of the night, not without at least letting us know he was there. Laughing at the sheer mystery of it all, I twirled around, imagining the wedding under the lights, my sister and her wife dancing together. It was going to be amazing. *This* was amazing.

As I twirled, I locked eyes with someone. Their eyes blinked, catching the light, but the figure remained in the shadows. My heart leaped, but I wasn't as terrified as I probably should have been, considering someone was lurking in the darkness of my backyard.

I stepped forward, half expecting the figure to retreat, to disappear entirely into the darkness. They didn't. They stayed still as I approached, one slow and careful step at a time. I was afraid to look away because I couldn't help but think that if I did, they wouldn't be there anymore. But they stayed, and as I drew closer, my eyes adjusted to the darkness, until at last the figure became clear.

He was about three feet tall. Unlike the cartoon drawings or knickknacks I'd seen, he wasn't chubby. There was no rounded belly, but instead a wall of solid muscle. Not defined, like someone who lifted weights, but *strong*, capable of carrying a great burden. Capable of doing pretty much whatever he wanted, probably.

His jaw was strong and his eyes were clear, deep-set under a heavy brow that made him look almost angry. But I still wasn't afraid.

"Are you . . . menehune?" I whispered.

He didn't answer; instead, he continued to stare at me, frowning. I stared back, trying to keep my face as calm and open as possible. *This* was what I'd been waiting for—a glimpse of the unseen, of the hidden things that Hilo had shown me still existed. More than anything in the world, I didn't want him to go away.

"Did you do this?" I asked, gesturing at the lights. In legends, menehune did things like this all the time, often completing enormous projects in a single night. I remembered my dad telling me the story of Laka, who made a feast for the menehune. In exchange, they crafted an entire canoe for him, hollowing out an enormous koa tree, carving and curing it and fashioning the ama, or outrigger. I wondered if perhaps this menehune had done us a similar favor, though I couldn't imagine why he would.

The menehune regarded me in thoughtful silence, then shook his head. He turned to leave, and my heart fell. Whatever I had been looking for was standing right in front of me, and he was walking away. No one would ever believe that it had happened. I shivered and held my shoulders more tightly, trying to be grateful to have had even just this encounter, this brief brush with the impossible and forgotten.

The menehune moved into the forest until I could barely see him at all, his figure melding into the brush—and then he stopped. I held my breath. He gave an annoyed sigh—the first sound I'd heard from him—and waved his hand in a curt gesture. It was an invitation of sorts. Apparently, I was supposed to follow him.

I tried not to think about how it was after midnight. I tried not to think about how I was in my pj's and was wearing grocery-store slippers.

I tried not to think about how worried my parents would be if they found me gone.

I tried not to think at all as I followed him, plunging into the darkness of the trees.

CHAPTER SEVEN

It was a long, cold trek. Despite his short legs, the menehune moved much faster than I did, leaping across logs and scrambling up slippery, leaf-strewn hills. Just as it had with Hilo, the forest seemed to move aside for him. Once again, it didn't seem particularly inclined to do that for me, but I did find that if I stayed close to the menehune, the going was a little easier, as if just my proximity to him made the trees offer their assistance. Unfortunately, this meant that I had to basically jog to keep up with him, but at least moving quickly kept me from feeling the cold as much.

I lost all sense of direction in the dark. Occasionally, I could see flashes of stars when there was a break in the trees, but there wasn't much of a moon, and I had no way of knowing where we were going. Somehow, my eyes adjusted enough that I could make out details that would have been visible only beneath the light of the fullest of moons—particularly if I stayed close to the menehune. It wasn't clear if this was something he was causing intentionally or just a side effect of being in his presence.

We emerged from the forest out onto a road, and the menehune walked gingerly across the black pavement. It took a moment for me to recognize where we were, though I'd certainly been spending a lot of time there lately. But here we were, crossing Wright Road. The menehune moved steadily without pause, but he seemed to shudder with every step it took to get across.

When we'd finally made it, I followed the menehune along the path to Hilo's shelter. He lay there sleeping, curled up against the cold. He was snuggled into the sleeping bag I'd given him and had also piled ferns over his body to serve as a sort of blanket.

"He's the one who did it?" I whispered to the menehune. "Hilo hung the lights for us?"

The menehune gave a brief nod.

I imagined Hilo clambering up into the trees in my backyard, stringing the twinkle lights while we were cozy inside. He probably hadn't even thought to use a ladder.

I shivered, and the menehune frowned at me. "Are you cold?" he asked abruptly.

I blinked at him. "You can talk? I mean, in English?"

"It's been the most common language in Hawai'i for over a hundred years," he said, rolling his eyes. "We've picked it up."

We? I thought. *There are more of you?* But it seemed kind of rude to ask something like that.

"Are you cold?" he repeated.

"Hang on," I said, any chill I might have been feeling completely forgotten. "If you can talk, why didn't you just *tell* me Hilo was the one who hung the lights, rather than make me hike all this way?"

"If you weren't willing to walk to know, it wasn't worth knowing," he replied.

I groaned and covered my face with my hands. Hilo stirred at the sound but didn't wake up. "This was a test?"

The menehune inclined his head.

"Look," I said. "I know what an honor this is, you coming to me and speaking with me. And I'm so grateful, really I am, and I promise I will do all that I can to live up to . . . I don't know, whatever it was that made you decide I was worth talking to. But we're a long way from home and it's late and it's cold and my parents are going to *freak out*."

The hike home was a lot faster. I don't know what the menehune did, but the forest cleared out of our way even more effectively than it had before. It seemed like the logs burrowed down into the dirt to make it easier to climb over them, and the trees appeared to even lean aside to allow a more direct path.

We made it back home, and I grabbed my dad's musty old raincoat from its hook in the garage and wrapped it around my shoulders, shivering.

"Thank you," I said. "For seeing me home, and for, you know, talking to me."

The menehune looked at me steadily. "You see us," he said abruptly. "You see the forest spirits, though you chose not to for a time."

I swallowed hard and nodded. "I didn't mean to choose not to. I wouldn't have, if I'd understood that was what I was doing. I was just..."

"You were young," the menehune finished. He studied me for another moment, then seemed to come to a decision. "The boy isn't really lōlō," he said. "He was made that way."

I stared at him, shocked. "You made Hilo go crazy?"

"Not me," he said defensively. "That's not something menehune do."

"So who did it, then?"

"The 'ōhi'a."

I remembered Hilo running from tree to tree, apologizing. "What on earth did he do to deserve that?" I demanded.

"Apparently, he carved his name into a tree outside Cooper Center."

"That's *all*?"

The menehune shrugged. "He harmed the tree. It was angry."

"He's just a dumb teenage boy! Do you *know* the kinds of stupid things teenage boys do? They can get a lot worse than that! This doesn't seem like maybe an overreaction to you?" I heard my voice rising and forced myself to calm down. The last thing I wanted was to wake my parents.

72

"If it *had* been me who punished him, he would have been turned to stone, so I think perhaps he should be grateful."

I gaped at him, unable to speak. I didn't want to be disrespectful, because let's face it, I definitely didn't want to be turned to stone for my insolence. Hilo had done a harmful thing, it was true, but to lose his sense of himself, to be so frightened and alone because of one foolish action—and to learn that it had been done *on purpose*, by the 'ōhi'a of all things, a being I had been taught to revere and protect. I was so angry I was shaking. I turned away to go back inside, to go wake up my parents and tell them about the boy I'd found in the woods, to put an end to this before he got hurt any further.

"Emma, wait." The menehune moved to stand in front of me, blocking my way. "We need your help. Yours and the boy's. So few people can see or hear us, and we need your help. The forest is being lost. We will have nowhere to go."

I crossed my arms. "Cursing people to make them crazy isn't a very good way of getting them to help you."

"I told you; we aren't responsible for that. And anyway, the curse is the only reason he can see us."

"Even if you aren't responsible, I bet you can fix it," I argued.

"Probably," the menehune admitted. "But if I'm going to help him, I want your help in return."

I narrowed my eyes at him. "This is why you came here tonight, isn't it? For some kind of help exchange?"

"That's what life on the islands is now, isn't it?" he replied flatly. "Just a series of exchanges and transactions. Nothing is for free."

I looked away, unable to argue with that. "Fine," I said. "But first you help Hilo."

The menehune nodded. "Agreed. You have my word."

"What is your name?" I didn't know if it was rude to ask—some cultures put a lot of stock in names, and Hawaiians are no exception—but apparently he knew my name, and it seemed disrespectful to just keep thinking of him as "the menehune."

"I am Koa," he said with a small smile. "I will find you both tomorrow." With that, he took a step backward, melting away into the shadows. My gifted night vision faded, and there was no evidence he'd ever been there at all.

It was past noon when I woke up. Mom must have been feeling really guilty about the whole hydrangea thing to let me sleep so late. I came out of my bedroom, yawning, to find a cold plate of banana pancakes resting on the table next to a note that read, "Went to Hilo, dentist appointment. Love you."

I made myself a cup of tea while the pancakes were heating up in the microwave. I wrapped half of them in a napkin to take over to Hilo and made him a thermos of tea to go with it. I forced myself to sit down and pour the syrup and use a knife and fork and drink my tea slowly so I didn't scald my tongue. It took every shred of self-control I had to prevent myself from racing out of there to go make sure the menehune had helped Hilo, but it was late enough in the day that a few more minutes wouldn't matter. It would probably be a long day, and I'd already had a long night—I needed to eat something. Not to mention Mom's pancakes were so good it would be a shame to scarf them.

I washed my dishes just in case Mom came home while I was gone, and then packed up to go. It was one of those bright Volcano days, when the green of the sugi pines stood out against the bright blue of the cloudless sky, like a saturation filter had been pushed to the limit on the whole world. It was also much warmer than usual, and I was sweating by the time I made it to Hilo's trail.

When I got there, I found that he'd placed a welcome mat on the side of the road, one of the scratchy brown ones you get at home improvement stores, saying *Bless This House*. Which was ironic, given that I was being welcomed to bushes and not a house at all.

I had the feeling Hilo wasn't entirely cured yet.

He heard the crackle of leaves and branches beneath my feet and looked up with a smile. "Girl!" he said. "Welcome!"

"Yeah, I saw that." I sat down next to him on his log and handed him the pancakes and tea. "Did you steal it?"

Hilo happily unwrapped the pancakes and folded one of them up like a burrito to shove into his mouth. He didn't answer, and I gave a shrug. "Well, I guess it's good that you're trying to make the place homey. Did, um, did anybody come by to visit you this morning?"

"You did."

"Yeah, but anybody else?"

Hilo looked at me blankly, and I sighed in resignation. I guess the menehune wasn't in a big rush to help Hilo, despite his promises. There was a rustling sound beside us, and I turned to see a curl of fern, waving and bobbing, almost like it was dancing.

"That's right; I remember that," Hilo said. He turned to me. "They say menehune come out only at night. We are to meet him tonight."

Was that true? I tried to think back to the legends I'd heard over the years. Heiau, or temples, as well as fishponds and roads—in the stories, all of them had been built by menehune in the space of a single night. It hadn't occurred to me that meant they were not in fact capable of being out in the day, but I supposed it made a certain amount of logical sense. It would have been nice of Koa to mention that, but I guess maybe he figured I already knew. And anyway, apparently, he'd sent a fern messenger with a reminder. Why not.

"What time tonight?"

Hilo conferred with the fern. "Dusk," he said. "Just as soon as the sun has gone down. He will be here."

CHAPTER EIGHT

IT WAS A NIGHT FOR COWS.

The mist had descended heavily, making it hard to see more than thirty feet ahead. It curled spookily, reaching forward like the breath of an unseen dragon. Which was all very atmospheric and lovely, in a Gothic sort of way, but the problem was, there was small herd of feral cows that tended to roam the village on misty evenings. When the fog rolled in, the cows went a-walking, leaving their pastures for the adventures of the lonely Volcano roads. If you were driving, you could come right up on one without warning, the fog clearing just as your headlights hit it, slamming your brakes and skidding across the wet asphalt. And let me tell you, cows are big. This was not a case where you hit the thing and figured you'd be fine. If it was you or the cow, my money was on the cow.

And since I was on my bike, it was definitely going to be the cow.

Trying to convince my parents that it was imperative that I leave for a bike ride right after dinner was a little challenging. I had to invent some kind of reasonable grounds for such an excursion, and all I could come up with was an emergency at Uncle Danny's store. Which was a terrible lie because it was so easily refuted, and therefore I would absolutely be catching hell for it later.

I shivered and hunched over the handlebars as the mist dripped down the back of my jacket collar. The leader of the herd, a giant milk-white steer, let out a bellow, and I knew he was close by, even if I couldn't see him. We are taught as toddlers that cows say "moo." And sure, sometimes they do. But this steer didn't moo. He roared like a particularly stentorious werewolf. A were-cow.

Logically I knew that he was just claiming his territory and protecting his herd. But in the eerie, low-lit mist, it was hard to stay logical.

I was grateful for Hilo's welcome mat, because in the darkness and without the menehune's guidance, I might have missed his trail otherwise. I hauled my bike off the road and switched on my flashlight to make sure I didn't trip over anything on the trail.

"Did you bring food?" Hilo asked.

"Of course I brought food," I said. "And it's not even peanut butter."

"But I like—"

"I know," I said patiently. "But you'll like this, too." I handed him the thermos, now filled with Portuguese bean soup—my dad's specialty. Hilo eyed it suspiciously, but it was warm and he was soaked. Ferns didn't tend to provide that much in the way of weatherproofing.

When he'd finished eating, I patted his knee, covered as it was in his filthy jeans. "With any luck, this will be your last night out here," I said encouragingly.

"It might take a little bit longer than that." I jumped at the sound of Koa's voice. I swear, he just materialized right there in front of us. No menehune, and then all of a sudden—menehune. "Come," he said.

Hilo stood to follow him, no questions asked. With a sigh, I closed the thermos and stuck it into the deep pockets of my raincoat. "Where are we going?" I asked.

The menehune didn't deign to answer, which I suppose I should have expected. As before, so long as I stayed reasonably close to him or to Hilo, the forest seemed to lean aside to let me pass. We didn't go far, and in fact, when we got where we were going, it made perfect sense— because I recognized this place. I had been here just once before, tromping around the woods with Mālie. It was a giant 'ōhi'a tree, likely around four or five hundred years old. It had scattered aerial roots hanging down like wiry red beards, its small, rounded leaves a dark gray-green. Its lower branches were entirely covered in moss, and it was a walking tree, meaning that its main trunk had grown horizontally and then sprouted smaller trees atop it, which then developed "legs" that reached toward the ground. It wasn't just a tree; it was a community, with 'ōlapa, painiu,

ʻalaʻala wai nui, kupukupu, and ʻiwaʻiwa growing on it, and lots of other trees, ferns, and mosses I didn't even know the names for.

Trees like this one didn't used to be rare. They were the spine of the forest, keeping it strong and holding the ecosystem together. But there were now so few of them, and this one grew on that tract of land under development, which meant that any day now, it was probably going to be cut down, its roots ripped up and the life it sustained cut off.

Koa climbed up onto the horizontal trunk and sat down comfortably, nestling himself in a crook between branches. Hilo and I stayed respectfully on the ground.

"Um . . . what happens now?" I asked after we'd been standing there in silence for several minutes.

Hilo took a deep breath and stepped up to the tree, exhaling onto an aerial root that dripped down toward the forest floor. "I'm sorry," he whispered. "E kala mai."

Koa snorted. "Well, no wonder the ʻōhiʻa is still mad at you. What, you harm one of his children and all you have to say is 'Oops, my bad'?" It was very odd to hear a menehune say *my bad*, even if it was said sarcastically. He caught my look, and I blushed. "What?"

"It's just, um, you don't sound very . . ."

"What?" he repeated, impatient.

"Magical," I mumbled.

Koa gave a short, sharp laugh. "Yes, well. We're not *elves*. We don't speak in poetry and glitter like starlight or whatever nonsense humans make up about forest folk. We're not the stories you've told about us. We're just people, trying to exist in a world that no longer welcomes us."

"But what else is Hilo supposed to do?" I demanded, trying to cover up my embarrassment. "He can't uncarve his name. It was a wrong thing to do, and he gets that. He's *really, really sorry*."

"Hoʻoponopono," Koa said. "He can make it right. If there is ʻeha, if you have caused harm, then it is your kuleana to do the work to fix it."

Hilo had dropped down, squatting on his heels in the wet beneath the tree, his head buried in his arms. I knelt beside him and tried to think how to explain it to him, when he had drifted so far away from language and understanding.

"When you carved the tree, you made it vulnerable to attack," I told him as gently as I could. "You're from Hilo, so you probably didn't know, but there's a fungus that's been killing the ʻōhiʻa. It can get in through any wound the tree receives."

"Make it right," Hilo whispered.

I sighed. "I don't know how you can do that. The fungus will get in, or it won't. I don't think there's anything you can do to stop it now."

"There isn't," Koa said. "But you *can* prevent further harm from coming to the ʻōhiʻa. Stop that development. Stop them from cutting down the forest."

I stared up at him, aghast. "How? He's just one boy! How can anyone do that? He doesn't have control over any of this!"

Koa stood up and jumped down from the 'ōhi'a, landing with a firm step. "Oh, nobody expects him to do it alone. But every move he makes toward being helpful will bring him back to himself." He glared at Hilo. "Ideally, he will remember this lesson."

I managed to haul myself out of bed by eight a.m., in time to enjoy breakfast while it was still hot. My dad was just pouring himself some coffee and sitting down with the paper. I helped myself to some scrambled eggs and made my version of coffee—milk, sugar, and probably about a tablespoon of coffee. I took a sip as I sat down at the table and choked.

Hilo's face was on the front page of the newspaper.

"That is so sad," my mom said. "Those poor people." She reached over to ruffle my hair. "I don't know what I would do if anything ever happened to you."

"It says he was last seen here in Volcano," Dad said. "Apparently, his father is one of the workers at the construction site up on Wright Road, and the kid was hanging out at Cooper Center while he was working—that's his last known location."

I scooped up some scrambled eggs with a shaking hand.

My mom dropped her fork with a clatter. "Are you serious? Right here in the village?" She turned to me. "Emma, no more going out after dark. Or wait, this happened during the day? In that case, I don't want you going out at all; do you understand me?"

I tried to calibrate the right tone of whining that I would ordinarily have under these circumstances if, you know, I didn't feel completely responsible for this missing person. "Mom, it's summer! And all I've been doing this whole time is working on wedding stuff!"

My dad lowered the paper and gave my mom a Look. They had a tacit agreement not to directly contradict each other but instead gave each other Looks that spoke volumes— and Dad is always the softer touch. "Fine," my mom said, giving up. "Fine! But no more after dark. Home for dinner every night, no matter what emergency my brother needs you for. Okay?"

I nodded emphatically, but my stomach fell. There was no way I was going to be able to do everything I needed to do during the day. Menehune came out only at night, and frankly, without Koa's guidance, I was at a bit of a loss.

I rushed through my wedding-related chores (cutting away dead ginger that *I would have sworn* I had already cut back) and headed out to find Hilo as soon as I could. When I got there, I found Hilo watching the bulldozing— or rather, the not-bulldozing, because the machine was broken again.

"Did you do that?"

He wouldn't look at me. "Make it right," he said, by way of explanation.

I exhaled a sigh of frustration. I didn't think this kind of sabotage was likely to make anything right, but I could see that he was in a tough position. I planted myself in front of him, forcing him to look at me. "Hilo, you have to go home. Your parents are looking for you, okay? Everyone is worried about you, and I should have made you go home that first day. I know you probably don't get this, but it was a really terrible thing I did, not telling anyone about you. Please, let's get out of here, get you back home and safe. Then we can figure all of this out, I promise."

"Can't," he said. "Not until . . ." He gestured at himself. "Not until I'm me."

That night, I didn't even try to come up with an excuse. There really wasn't any reason I could invent that would persuade my mom to let me go out after dark, so I just sneaked out after my parents had gone to bed. I didn't feel good about it, but I didn't feel like I had a choice, either.

When I made it to the construction site, I found Hilo and Koa absolutely laying waste to all the equipment. They were ripping hoses, jamming gears, and pouring water in places water wasn't supposed to go. Spark plugs were being hurled about like popcorn, and there was a wide variety of clangs and thunks indicating that Very Bad Mechanical Things were happening. It was like a really destructive buddy movie.

I jogged into the field and placed myself in Koa's path, crossing my arms. "All right, what's going on?" I demanded. "There is no way all of this is about one 'ōhi'a tree."

Koa crossed his arms over his thick chest. "Why would you just throw your trash into the forest?" I stared at him blankly, and he snorted. "You don't even remember. Well, you did. You threw your broken junk into the forest, like our home was just your own personal garbage heap."

I felt the blood drain from my face. "The broken mug. You're the one who's been sabotaging my sister's wedding, aren't you? Why? It's not her fault, or my mom's—I was the one who did that."

He nodded tightly. "So you were. You have some ho'oponopono to do, too. You and Hilo both."

"All right, I . . ." I pushed my hair out of my eyes, sighing. "I understand. Just, please don't screw around with the wedding anymore, okay? You can't just go around breaking human stuff! Look at that excavator! I'm not happy about any of this, either," I said, gesturing to the fallen trees and upturned earth all around us. "But, like, it happens. People come here and they build things. It sucks, but it's inevitable. Messing with them isn't going to make them just *go away*."

Hilo tapped me on the shoulder. I shrugged him off, but when he tapped again, more urgently, I rounded on him, exasperated. "What?!"

He pointed, and my heart stuttered in my chest. There, at the edge of the forest, stood menehune. And not just one, but dozens of them—men, women, and even children. They were all just as compact and strong as Koa, and when they moved, I couldn't hear a thing. They had walked through the forest like ghosts.

All I could do was stand there, staring at them. I think I probably would have stayed frozen there all night, but Hilo gently took my hand in his and led me over to them. Koa walked beside us, and then he went and stood with his people. We stood facing them at the edge of the devastation, with only the moonlight to see by, and I felt tears prick my eyes. They looked so vulnerable, gathered there in the darkness, and yet at the same time so incredibly strong and resilient.

One of them stepped forward. She looked younger than Koa, though I wasn't entirely clear on how to determine menehune age. This menehune was an adult ... ish? She looked young, somehow, but with the body of an adult. She wore an old sweatshirt sized for a human, but she, or someone else, had cut out the neck and the cuffs and in their place had braided in some twisted tī leaves. The sweatshirt was printed with ferns and dyed with splotches of blossoms. It was simultaneously functional and startlingly beautiful. She said, "Koa, this is a mistake."

Our menehune frowned at her. "Lanakila, we have discussed this, and I have made my decision. They are welcome here. If you trust me, trust them."

The girl, Lanakila, looked as though she wasn't particularly sure she trusted anything at all, but she nodded. "You are the chief."

I stared at Koa in disbelief. "You're the chief?"

Koa shrugged. "I suppose. There aren't really enough of us to warrant a full system of government, but—"

"You are our leader," Lanakila finished for him. "And so, we obey you." I could hear an unspoken *for now* in her tone, but if Koa noticed it, he was prepared to ignore it.

"Come," he said to Hilo and me.

The menehune moved in a procession, and while the detritus of the forest crackled beneath our feet, the menehune moved silently—even the children were startlingly quiet. One of them crept up and reached out for me. He was so low to the ground that I had to stoop a little to hold his hand; his palm small and warm. My other hand squeezed Hilo's—we hadn't let go—and as he smiled at me, I saw that he was leaning down, holding the hand of an even younger menehune child. I didn't know what had made Hilo and me worthy of this kind of trust. We were strangers here among these people, and yet their children reached out to us. It was a gift, and for all the complaining I'd been doing up to that moment, I knew that I wanted to live up to their faith in us.

As we walked, Koa explained to us how the menehune had stayed hidden for so long. They had gone underground—literally. Instead of making their homes in the forest, they now lived in a lava tube. These tubes are formed when flowing lava crusts over, creating a kind of lid that seals in the heat, allowing the liquid lava beneath it to stay hotter and therefore move faster until it pours out to the surface. When it does, it ends up leaving behind a kind of subway tunnel, often stretching for miles. The Big Island is riddled with them, like enormous worm trails beneath the surface, the ground hollow below our feet. Some of them, like Nāhuku lava tube, are electrified and open to the public, but most are pitch black, with only the occasional entrance or rockfall-created skylight providing illumination.

The entrance to the lava tube where the menehune lived was so small and hidden by overgrowth that I'd never noticed it, even after all the time I'd spent rambling around these woods. But once we got inside, it opened up into a grand space, with cathedral ceilings dotted with tiny stalactites. The lava rock was worn as smooth as concrete by the speed of the lava that had flowed through years and years before. There were roots reaching down from the ceiling and cleverly hidden skylights that provided some starlight.

I couldn't believe *what* I was seeing. It wasn't what I would have imagined, based on the stories, but then what would it be like to be a forest people, now, in the age of grocery stores and strip malls? The menehune had furnished the lava tube using couches whose stuffing was ripped and stained, yet still comfortable. They had pillows, blankets, broken lawn chairs, even a rusted wheelbarrow. An old sink was being used to collect water that dripped down through a crack in the lava-tube ceiling. There were chipped dishes and glass jars, old beer bottles and plastic garden planters. A broken stop sign sat horizontally atop a rock, serving as a kind of table. I blushed to see the broken mug I'd tossed into the bushes outside Cooper Center, placed now at the center of the stop sign, filled with wildflowers. It was as if the Borrowers had gone shopping at the local garbage dump. They had found a way to make use of every single thing, making the broken not only functional, but comfortable.

And somehow, despite how scavenged and practical everything was, it was also beautiful. The handles of the wheelbarrow were intricately carved, with geometric designs that echoed the movement of the winds through the trees, the curl of a fern, the jagged edge of a rock. These same designs had been stamped onto dyed cloths that hung around the curved walls of the lava tube, and in the gaps between the tapestries, there were labyrinthine mosaics of broken glass pressed into the walls. Jars of various herbs and liquids swung from the ceiling, like a hanging apothecary.

Natural shelves of lava rock were piled high with pillows and blankets, like bunk beds. The little menehune child who had walked with me tugged at my hand, showing me where he slept. His bed was made of old towels, all of them piled up and folded neatly together and covered with a delicate and cozy quilt made of various knitted squares, cut from what I guessed were old sweaters, all sewn together. He had a small stuffed elephant tucked into his makeshift bed, and my heart squeezed inside my chest in recognition. That elephant had been mine, but I'd lost it years ago in this same forest. At the time I'd cried, but now I felt only relief and gratitude that my elephant had found someone else who would love him.

The incongruity and startling beauty of it all made me want to stop and look at everything, but Koa led Hilo and me farther into the lava tube. As we wandered through, I could see places where the menehune worked, including giant wooden calabashes for pounding poi and salting fish. I saw the 'ohe kāpala, the carved bamboo stamps that they used to dye the kapa cloth they made from tree bark. Some areas were clearly used for storing food and tools, including broken but still usable shovels and machetes. We walked on and on, following Koa, until eventually we came to a block in the tunnel. There had been a rockfall, and it was clear that it had happened recently. Large and small boulders were scattered across the cave floor, and when I looked up at the ceiling, I could see the jagged, fresh gaps that had been left when they fell.

"We lost three menehune when the ceiling collapsed," Koa said. He spoke quietly, but his voice echoed in the stillness. "It's the digging. They're tearing up the roots and jackhammering into the rock. As they move farther into the forest"—he gestured behind him—"they will be digging above where we live. Where the children are. And then the roof will fall, and more will die."

I gaped at him, horrified. "Then you have to leave! You have to get them out of here, right now!"

Koa shook his head. "That's impossible."

"But—"

He shook his head again, firm and implacable. "It cannot be done. We have a sacred duty here. We protect this forest, and we cannot leave it. So you see now why this development must be stopped."

I exchanged a look with Hilo, and I could see the resolve in his eyes—a resolve that had been there even before we understood *why*. Yes, clearly the development had to be stopped.

But knowing that didn't help me understand *how*.

CHAPTER NINE

WE TRIED, OBVIOUSLY. HILO SPENT most of the next day clearing any ginger and uluhe that were choking ʻōhiʻa trees, along with continuing his sabotage of the worksite. I put up signs protesting the construction all over the village, including at the garbage dump, the post office, and, of course, Uncle Danny's store. I even taped a big banner to Uncle Mike's tow truck. (I had two nights left before I had promised Ana I would tell someone about Hilo, and the deadline was making me a little manic.)

I think my parents were a little taken aback by such uncharacteristic activism. We had waved signs on the side of the highway for various local political candidates my entire life, but I had always done so under protest. I organized a rally of sorts; I guilted all my family members into going, which all together was basically half the village. Uncle Danny closed the store for the day, and he and Auntie Paula brought some people from their church. Uncle Mike didn't attend the rally, as he'd been doing work at the site repairing equipment we had sabotaged, and he said it felt awkward to protest something he was receiving money from—which was fair enough. Auntie Carol and their kids came, though. Ikaika and his family were there, as was the postmaster and Auntie Mele from Cooper Center—and Auntie Mele had her crochet, of course. The lady who sells all the fruit at the farmers' market was there, and she'd brought rambutan and ice cream bean pods and loquat for everyone to snack on. We set up lawn chairs, and the little kids brought bikes and skateboards and rode around in circles, avoiding the cow patties in the road.

Clean Jeans, the manager guy, came over to demand our permit, which I triumphantly presented (my parents had helped me apply for it).

"You know this is pointless, yeah?" he sneered. He wasn't talking to me, of course, but to my mother—because who would ever think a lowly teenager capable of community organization? "We have the full green light from the county and the state. This land is bought and paid for."

My dad came and stood beside my mom and me. "It's still worth making a point."

Clean Jeans eyed my dad, then grudgingly held out his hand. "Hey, Joe, how's it going."

"Aloha, Kainoa." They shook hands, and my dad shrugged at me. "We went to high school together."

Of course they did. Everybody in Hawaii went to high school together.

Clean Jeans—Kainoa, I guess—frowned down at me. "I don't suppose you know anything about the problems we've been having with our machinery?" he asked me. I guess teenagers are more plausible when it comes to vandalism.

"Is that an accusation?" Dad asked mildly.

Kainoa put up his hands. "Nope. Just, you know, asking."

"So who is your employer?" Dad asked. "The records list a company on the mainland I didn't recognize."

Kainoa shrugged. "Yeah, it's this corporation with a bunch of high-end resorts and retreats in California and the Southwest."

"You always were pushing for the islands to 'embrace the future,' even when we were in school," my dad said.

"Eh, it'll be good for the community, you know," Kainoa said, a note of defensiveness in his voice. "Trees aren't jobs. They aren't tax revenue. Look at these roads," he said, pointing at the cracks in the asphalt, at the places where the jungle had grown over the pavement. "The county will finally have to fix all of this. Maybe you'll even get on the grid, be able to get water out here. Maybe there will be mail delivery and you won't have to go to the post office."

"We don't *want* any of that!" I said. "We live out here because this is how we like it!"

Would it have been nice to be able to rely on always having enough water to wash the dishes and take a shower even in a drought? Yes. Would it be nice to be able to drive on a road without worrying about the undercarriage of your car? Sure. Or what about being able to order perfume and other things that often won't ship to a PO box? Absolutely. But *not* having all those things meant that instead we could hear birdsong instead of street traffic, with the wind whistling through the ironwood trees and the distant barking of dogs. We could walk down the side of the road and wave at every single car that passed by and know that even if somebody got your address wrong, the postmaster would put it in the correct box anyway, because they *knew you.*

I had no idea how I could even begin to explain any of this to Kainoa, but before I could try, there was a deafening clanging, louder even than the ongoing bulldozer noises, and I jumped. Kainoa turned around to look, gave a shout, and began running. After a moment's hesitation, I followed, running after him, with half the village behind me.

Someone had turned on the excavator and was using the bucket to smash and tear at the bulldozer. It looked like a Transformers battle sequence in extreme slow motion. The excavator ripped at the bulldozer's giant tire, and the metal gave a shrieking, painful shudder. There was shouting and men were running everywhere, all of them racing toward the excavator. There was so much happening that at first I couldn't tell what was going on, but then I saw—it was Hilo. Hilo was driving the excavator.

A construction worker jumped onto the side of the excavator and pulled himself up, even though it was still in motion. There was a bit of a tussle, and then the excavator turned off. There were so many people crowded in front of me, but as I craned my neck to see what was going on, I saw the man who had pulled himself onto the machine throw his arms around Hilo. They were both sobbing.

The rally broke up after that, and it became clear that the man was Hilo's dad. Hilo had been at the skate park the day I met him because he'd been bored while his dad was at work, and so he had come to hang out in Volcano.

I stood on the sidelines and watched as Hilo's father held his crying son, tears running down his own face. When he looked up, Hilo and I made eye contact. He held my gaze as if he didn't ever want to look away from me, like I was the only one who could understand what was happening. But he didn't say anything, and neither did I. What could I say in that moment, with everyone shouting about calling the police and child services? I just stood and watched as his dad, understandably emotional, led him to a car to take him home.

There was no chance for goodbyes. What would we have even said? As I watched them drive away, I realized I didn't even know his name. Sure, I could have figured it out easily enough—all I would have had to do was read the newspaper article about the missing boy. But I had avoided the news and rumors about his disappearance. Deep down, I knew it would have meant confronting how horrible a person I was hiding him from his terrified family. But it was more than that. Not knowing who he really was meant I could keep him as just Hilo, my boy in the forest, my guide to a more magical world.

That was over now. I was glad he was going home, I truly was, but suddenly I felt so alone. He was the only other person who knew what was going on beneath the local politics and the ever-present dance between progress and preservation—only we seemed to recognize that this forest was a microcosm of the erosion of the spirituality of Hawai'i, its sacred truths that had survived by hiding underneath everyday life, like a vein of silver ore beneath the rocks. Hilo had been the only person I could talk to about any of this, even if he didn't make much sense most of the time.

What was going to happen to him now? How was he going to get well? How was he going to work to make things right if he was in Hilo? How was he going to explain any of this to his parents? How would I explain it to mine?

When his dad's car was finally out of sight, I turned around and found my parents looking at me.

"Emma," my mom said quietly. "Get in the car, please."

They didn't say anything to me on the short drive home. We got out of the car, and I sat down at the kitchen table while my mom made herself a cup of tea. My dad put away his phone, and my mom sat down opposite me, blowing on her tea to cool it down. "You've been sneaking out at night," she said at last.

I drew on the table with my fingernail, following the pattern of math homework I'd carved into it years ago when

I forgot to put a magazine underneath. I nodded, my throat so tight I couldn't speak.

"And you knew that boy? The one who was missing? You were going to see him?"

I nodded again.

"Emma, I don't understand," my mom said. "Why wouldn't you tell anyone about him? Why would you lie to us?"

"He needed my help," I said quietly.

"Helping him would have been getting him home!" My mom took a deep breath, willing herself to calm down. "This doesn't make any sense."

"I know." I felt my eyes fill with tears, and I tried to blink them away. "I'm sorry."

"Emma," Dad said. "What is going on?"

I looked up at them, finally. They didn't look mad, exactly—just really, really worried. "I don't know if you'll believe me," I said in a small voice.

"Try us," Mom said.

I took a deep breath. "Okay." I tried to think where to start. "You know how it's felt like the things we were doing, getting stuff ready for the wedding, it seemed like it was all being undone? Like, we would cross one task off the list, and in the morning it would be all messed up again?"

My mom nodded slowly.

"Well, it *was* getting messed up. We weren't imagining it. It was . . ." *Oh man, here we go,* I thought. "It was menehune."

For a moment, there was silence. And for a heartbeat, I thought maybe they would actually believe me, that even though what I was saying sounded completely ridiculous (and I did know that), they would still listen, because it was *me* talking, and they trusted me.

But then my dad pushed his chair back, scraping it loudly across the kitchen floor. "I'm going upstairs," he said flatly.

My mother sighed. "Joe . . ."

"If she's not interested in talking to us, I'm not interested in talking to her." I watched as he walked out of the room and up the stairs, the floorboards creaking overhead. Eventually, I heard the television turn on, the tinny voices of sports announcers drifting down through the floor.

After a moment, I said, "I'm not lying, Mom."

She took a last sip of her tea, then got up to rinse out the mug. "Emma, I don't know what to tell you. You did lie to us. You've lost our trust. And you expect me to believe *this*?"

I didn't have a response to that. I scrubbed the tears away with the back of my hand and got up and left the table.

CHAPTER TEN

I SHUT MYSELF UP IN MY BEDROOM. IN TRUTH, I didn't blame my parents for not believing me. I wouldn't have believed me, either. But it *was* the truth, and the menehune still needed help, and without Hilo—and without my parents—I felt frustrated and angry and helpless. I lay on my bed and stared at the glow-in-the-dark stars stuck to my ceiling. My mom and I had arranged them to mimic constellations, but we hadn't paid attention to the star map, so my guess was they looked like some other part of the universe.

There was a knock on my door. I didn't want to answer—what else could my parents have to say to me besides how disappointed they were or how irresponsible and careless I'd been? I knew all of that, and I didn't really want to hear it.

"Yeah?" I called after a moment.

"It's your sister," my dad said flatly.

I opened the door and took the phone from him, before closing it again.

"Okay, Emma, what happened?" she asked.

There was no anger in her voice, no disappointment or judgment—just a genuine desire to understand, and it broke through the wall of self-control I'd been trying too hard to keep from crumbling. I started to cry in earnest, and once I'd calmed down enough to speak clearly, I told her everything. I lay back down on my bed and told her about the lying, about finding Hilo in the woods, about the ʻōhiʻa, about Koa and all the menehune underground. Puʻulena didn't interrupt, not once. She didn't scoff or judge. She just listened, all the way through to the end.

When I finished, she sighed. "Wow, Emma."

"I know," I said, and wiped my eyes.

"Okay, first off, I believe you. I mean, I believe *something* happened—I don't know if it was menehune or what, but I believe that this was important to you, and that you did it all for a reason."

"Mom and Dad don't think that," I sniffed.

"Yeah, I know. Mom called to get me to talk to you, and she told me she didn't understand why you were lying."

I clenched my fists.

Puʻulena could hear my anger in my silence, like she always could. "To be fair, it was kind of messed up not to tell anyone about that boy. He could have been really hurt."

"But he had to stay in the woods so he could make amends to the ʻōhiʻa!" I said defensively.

"I know, Emma," Puʻulena said patiently. "But that's going to be hard for most people to understand, even Mom and Dad. It was dangerous, and to be honest, it does sound kind of crazy. Do you think he's okay now?"

"I don't know." I swallowed around the lump in my throat, thinking about how frightened Hilo had been, but how he had seemed more energized, even inspired, as he had worked his way toward ho'oponopono. "He was getting better, I think, but I don't know if he had done enough."

"Well, I think you'd better find out, don't you? What's his real name, anyway?"

"I don't know," I confessed. "It was in the newspaper article about how he was missing, but I kind of . . . ignored it."

"Oh my God, Emma, are you serious?" My sister sighed. "All right, I just googled him. For your information, your friend's name is Alika Kaneshiro, and he lives up Kaumana in Hilo. I couldn't get a phone number, but I have his address. Why don't you go see him, see how he's doing?"

"How?" I demanded. "Do you think Mom and Dad are going to, like, drive me to his house? I'm pretty sure I'm grounded. Also, I don't know if his parents know about me, but if they do, they probably hate me for not telling anyone I'd found their son."

There was a pause, and I could hear my sister tapping her fingernail against her teeth, something she always did when was thinking. I heard Naomi's voice in the background. "Naomi says hi," Pu'ulena said.

"I say hi, too," I replied, a little meekly.

"All right, here's the plan. If you tell Mom and Dad you want to apologize to Alika's parents, they'll let you off the hook with the grounding long enough to go do that. They'll probably even drop you off. Make this about taking personal responsibility. And," she added pointedly, "it has the added benefit of being the right thing to do."

I glared at the ceiling.

"You're welcome?" she said.

"Thank you," I said begrudgingly. I sat up and crossed my legs, hunching over a little. "I do appreciate it," I added quietly. "Especially that you believed me."

"I'll always believe you," she said. "I love you. And I'll see you soon! We'll be there in just a couple more weeks!"

"Yeah, and then you'll be *maaarried*," I said in a singsong voice.

"Not if Naomi doesn't clean the kitchen, I won't," she said sharply. "'Omi! Emma says you have to clean up!"

"I said absolutely no such thing. I don't know what it's about, but I'm definitely on Naomi's side."

I hear Naomi sing through the phone. "No, she doesn't; Emma loooooves me!"

Puʻulena laughed. "Busted! All right, I love you."

"I love you, too," I said. I hung up the phone and flopped back down onto the bed.

I knew that Puʻulena didn't actually think I'd been hanging out with menehune, because nobody would—it sounded like nonsense, and I wouldn't have believed me, either. But when she said she believed me, what she really meant was that she *believed in me*, and that was enough. For now.

Miracle of miracles, my parents even agreed to drop me off at Ana's house for the day after I'd finished my apology visit to Hilo's . . . I mean, Alika's, house. My mom made it clear that allowing me to spend time with Ana wasn't intended as a reward—it was because she was concerned that my isolation over the summer, working so hard on the wedding and not seeing my friends, had led to an overactive imagination and some bad decision-making, and Ana was a sensible girl who would set me straight. (She didn't say any of that out loud, but that was the gist.) But first things first.

As we pulled up outside the address Puʻulena had given me, Mom told me that she was going to run errands and would come pick me up in thirty minutes. That was probably enough time for me to make my apologies, get yelled at, apologize some more, and then leave.

I swallowed hard as she drove off. Yeah, this was going to be *awesome*.

I walked up to the door, my feet heavy. I had wanted to make a good impression, so I'd dressed up in the pretty empire-waisted gown I'd bought because it made me feel like I lived in Jane Austenland. It had a high collar and a not-insignificant quantity of ruffles, and I had felt good about myself when I left the house. But it was always so *hot* in Hilo, and the fabric stuck to my chest. I wiped my forehead and told myself it was the heat and humidity that was making me sweat. Definitely not nerves.

Hilo's house wasn't fancy, but it was very nice, with a small porch at the front door and a yard in front and behind. There was tī planted in the corners of the property and a yellow hibiscus growing near the front steps. I could smell a gardenia, though I couldn't see it.

I walked up the steps, avoiding squashing the moss that grew in the cracked cement. There was a screen door, and it squeaked as I pulled it open so I could knock on the main door. A dog immediately started barking, and I jumped. It sounded *big*, and it was loud.

"Eh!" I turned around to find a local man leaning out the window next door. "Why you making that dog all huhū?"

"Oh! Um, I'm sorry. I was just coming by to see Mr. and Mrs. Kaneshiro."

"I've never seen you before. You don't live around here. What business you have with them? They've been through a lot already."

I swallowed hard, feeling guilt pool in my stomach. "I know. I'm—"

"The last thing they need is for some haole girl to come bother them. In Hawai'i, we don't just show up at someone's house uninvited."

"I know. I'm not—"

"You people from the mainland, you think it's okay to just do what you like, go where you want. It's not right."

I felt the sting of tears behind my eyes. My heart was racing. "I know. Like I said, I'm not—"

"You leave these poor people alone. They no stay anyway; they had to take da kine to the doctor, make sure he's all right."

At that, the tears spilled over. Because of course they needed to do that, of course Hilo had to go to the doctor—he was probably malnourished and dehydrated. I nodded quickly and closed the screen door, which squeaked again, which of course made the Kaneshiros' dog start up again. I turned and ran down the stairs, out onto the sidewalk, and down the street.

But I had nowhere to go. I pulled out my phone to call my mom to come get me, but it was dead because I'm a thoughtless person and I forgot to charge it. Hilo wasn't home, and I couldn't possibly go back and sit there and wait for him to come back, not with that man hanging out the window to yell at me. I kept running until I had rounded the corner, where I sat down on the curb to let myself cry a little.

I was mad at myself and frustrated by the man. I understood how he felt, and how it must have seemed. Someone he didn't know coming to bother them, when their son had just been missing? He was just trying to protect his neighbors.

But he didn't have to tell *me* how to behave in Hawaiʻi. I was born and raised here. I was part Hawaiian, even if I didn't look or sound like it.

What does "looking Hawaiian" even mean, anyway? I glanced down at my outfit, feeling stupid. No one in Hawaiʻi dressed like this. I should've known better. But the worst part was my voice. I *sounded* like someone from the mainland. I didn't have a local accent. I didn't speak pidgin.

It was hardly the first time someone didn't know I was Hawaiian. Kids at school didn't believe me when I told them—they laughed and said I was lying, or worse, they patronizingly explained to me the difference between being *from* Hawai'i and being kanaka maoli, of Hawaiian descent.

Why didn't I just say something? Why didn't I tell the man, "I'm *not* from the mainland. I'm Hawaiian." It probably wouldn't have mattered, anyway—I knew from experience that saying I was Hawaiian wouldn't change anything about how people perceived me. I had a Native Hawaiian trigonometry teacher who one day during class went on a rant about colonization and pointed at me and Ana and our friends, the ones who sat in the front row and did particularly well in his class, and told us that we haoles should "get off his island." I ran out of class as soon as the bell rang, hurt for not being seen as Hawaiian, but also hurt *as a Hawaiian*, that we couldn't see ourselves in someone who was studious and did well in school. What did it say about what we had been told to believe about ourselves, the internalized racism of thinking that just because someone read a lot and was an admitted Anglophile, they couldn't also be Hawaiian? Couldn't also be proud of their heritage?

"Are you okay, honey? You want me to call someone for you?"

I looked up to see a kind-looking Hawaiian lady leaning over me. She wore a lauhala hat with flowers tucked into the brim, her hair graying but still long and waving down her back.

"I'm okay," I said, wiping my eyes. "Sorry."

She squeezed my shoulder. "Are you sure?"

I took a shuddering breath. "Yeah, I'm sure. Actually..." I glanced back toward Hilo's house. "Would it be all right if I called my mom?"

"Of course!" The woman rummaged in her bag, pulled out her phone, and handed it to me. My mom picked up right away.

"Mom, it's me."

"Emma? How did it go?"

"They weren't home," I said.

Mom must have heard something in my voice because she asked, "What's wrong?"

"Can you come get me?"

"Of course. I'm at Longs Drugs, but I'll be there in ten minutes. Okay?"

"Okay."

I handed the woman back her phone. "Thank you," I said. "She'll be here soon."

"No worries." She patted my shoulder again. "Everything will be fine. Will you be all right by yourself?"

I nodded. "I'm fine. Just... it's been a hard week."

The woman pulled me up to give me a hug, and she smelled like rice flour and the tuberose perfume my grandma used to wear before she died. With a last warm smile, she continued on her way.

My mom arrived in less than ten minutes, and when I climbed into the car, we sat there parked on the shoulder while I told her what happened. She was silent for a moment. She isn't Hawaiian, but she was born and raised on Oʻahu and has had her own struggles with belonging, with feeling accepted as someone who has lived here her entire life. At last, she sighed. "I'm sorry, honey. That shouldn't have happened. That man was probably just having a hard day, or maybe somebody was rude and presumptuous earlier, and he thought you would be the same."

"I know."

"I shouldn't have let you go there by yourself, to go see strangers. If I'd been there, I could have said something to him."

"I thought it was something I should do." I shrugged. "I guess I'll write the Kaneshiros a letter or something instead."

My mom reached over to squeeze my hand before she had to let go to turn on the car. "Well. Should we go pick up some manapua or something for you to take to Ana's?"

CHAPTER ELEVEN

ANA'S HOUSE RESTED ATOP A BLUFF WITH a view of the ocean, the grasses that grew in the wake of the defunct sugarcane industry angling down toward the sea. The house was octagonal, which made for interesting room shapes, and the entire western wall was made of glass, so when the sun set it was blinding, but in the best possible way. She had a couch made out of a clawfoot bathtub that had been cut in half and piled with throw pillows and lots of swinging hammock chairs, and pottery and ironwork art decorated the mustard-colored walls. It wasn't like any other house I'd ever seen, but it was so perfectly Ana and I loved it.

After my mom dropped me off, we said hello to Ana's dad, and I *thought* maybe he registered that I was there? It was hard to tell with him sometimes. One time he'd complimented Ana on her "new" shoes, which she'd worn every day for the past six months. I took off the ill-advised dress, exchanging it for a borrowed swimsuit. We took the manapua I'd brought and grabbed some star fruit and pickled mango and a couple of towels and headed off down the road. About a half mile from Ana's house we came to a small bridge that crossed high above the nearby Nānue Stream. It was just a one-lane road, and the bridge was even narrower, its rock-wall sides covered in moss and trees hanging over it into the road, their roots crumbling the pavement. Vegetation in Hawai'i is no joke. We climbed—well, slid—down the embankment alongside the bridge and slowly began rock hopping our way upriver. Ana preferred to go barefoot, but the riverbed could be sharp and a little mucky, so I kept my slippers on.

As we clambered upstream, climbing over boulders and occasionally wading in the water, I told Ana about the menehune, about what had happened to Hilo, and about trying to go see his family to apologize and getting yelled at by their neighbor instead. Ana thought for a long time before saying anything, which was always frustrating in the moment but ultimately something I appreciated about her. "I've always been a little jealous of you for being Hawaiian," she said at last.

I paused, balanced awkwardly between two rocks. "Why?"

She shrugged but didn't look at me, concentrating on climbing over a slippery boulder. "I don't know. Kids at school call me haole girl. . . ."

"They call me that, too," I pointed out.

"Yeah, but *you* know it's not true. You just don't tell them."

"Because when I do, they don't believe me," I muttered.

"That doesn't change the fact that it's true. I mean, yeah, you got in that argument with Jennifer Kekoa last year because she refused to accept that you're Hawaiian."

"Yeah, and that worked out so well for me," I said, rolling my eyes. "She gave me a hard time every day for a month after I had the temerity to stand up to her."

"So what?" Ana said, sounding annoyingly reasonable. "Jennifer Kekoa sucks. She's sucked since we were five. It's got nothing to do with whether you're Hawaiian enough or local enough or anything. It's just Jennifer Kekoa being Jennifer Kekoa."

I swatted a mosquito. "Jennifer Kekoa *is* very Jennifer Kekoa," I admitted.

"Exactly."

We finally arrived at the waterfall. It had been raining recently, so it was flowing hard, but not so hard that it felt unsafe—just enough to create a cascade of white that tumbled down from overhead. It wasn't very big, probably only fifteen or twenty feet up, but it was private and it was ours. I'd never seen anyone else here, not even once. I placed my towel onto a dry rock and jumped into the pool with a scream—it was *cold*. The water was a clearish brown, of course, being a tropical river, and we would definitely need to rinse off in Ana's outdoor shower after, but none of that mattered. Coming here always felt like washing away everything that I had brought with me, as if the river could just carry it all out to sea.

Once we had somewhat acclimated to the temperature (hot tip: dunk your head fully underwater to adjust faster), we set off at a stroke, swimming hard toward the waterfall. This isn't something I would have done at just any waterfall—there can be caves underneath, and you can get sucked under—but I knew from years of experience that this one was safe. Even so, there was always a sense of panic whenever we got close to the falls, the feeling that no matter how hard you swam, you were never going to make it. Then some invisible barrier would give way, and the waterfall would beat down on your back and shoulders, spiking your adrenaline, pushing you down—but then all of a sudden, you would have made it through. And then there was nothing but roaring and violent stillness.

There was just enough space to stand behind the wall of water, and Ana and I panted as we caught our breaths. It was dark behind the falls, and the spray fell in toward the wall instead of out, so we were constantly blinking our eyes clear. But there was also no pull, no tug of the river dragging you downstream. The water splashed but it didn't try to take us anywhere—we could stay as long as we wanted, here where there was nothing to see or hear except the crashing water.

On an impulse, I gave Ana a hug. "Thanks," I shouted over the thundering falls. "I needed this."

She squeezed me back, her arms wet and tight across my shoulders.

When we were too cold to stay in any longer, we laid out on boulders heated by the sun and ate our snacks. We talked about what it would be like to live in London, to wear knee-high leather boots and go to the Globe Theater and visit Poets' Corner in Westminster Abbey. We talked a little bit about Ana's crush on Benedict Cumberbatch because she had a problem and it was called Lanky British Men—not something commonly found in Hawaii.

Eventually we got kind of quiet, dangling our feet into the water and letting the ʻōpae nibble at our toes. We talked a little about her mom and the pressure Ana felt to always be the best at everything. And about her dad, who didn't always even notice she existed. I didn't have any good answers for her. I never did, but I said the same thing I always did—that her parents loved her (and they did; I was sure of it). That being kind of pushy, or being distracted a lot, didn't mean that love wasn't still there.

"I wish I could see things like you do. The menehune and the other creatures," Ana said. "It would be incredible to have that, something that wasn't about school or my parents or anything else about real life—something that was outside all of that, *bigger* than all of that."

I wasn't sure what to say, and I pulled my legs out of the water, turning over so the warmth of the rock would be on my stomach instead of my back. As I did, I saw something move out of the corner of my eye. I kept my gaze straight forward, allowing it to blur a little. There, rising up out of the water, was a moʻo, a lizard.

But somehow I knew that if I turned my head, it would be a rock once more.

"Ana," I whispered. "There's one right now. It's off to the right, just behind where we left the towels." As I spoke, I wondered if perhaps I shouldn't have—because what if she didn't see it? She'd never been able to before, and what if pointing it out now only made her feel worse? But as Ana slowly, ever so slowly, sat up to look, I saw her face change, and I knew that she could see it, too. I turned my head, and for once it didn't disappear and become a rock again. The moʻo was the size of a bicycle, and it stretched out one long clawed foot and then another, making its way upriver, unhurried, clambering over the rocks just as we had done. Its skin was bumpy and jagged—rocklike, but not rock. It paid no attention to us, but I knew that it was choosing to be seen, which meant it trusted us.

I bowed my head, and Ana followed suit. Eventually, it reached the pool beneath the waterfall, and it slipped under the surface, the arc of its spine barely visible above the water. It moved faster now that it was swimming. When it reached the wall on the other side of the pool, it climbed up, its body completely vertical, its claws gripping with precision and care as it made its way up alongside the waterfall, until at last it disappeared up over the edge.

For a moment, neither of us said anything. We just breathed.

"I don't understand," Ana whispered. "How . . . how could I see it? I thought it was just you."

I shrugged, bewildered. I certainly didn't have any answers.

"No, seriously." Ana turned to face me, wrapping her arms around her legs. "How does this work? Because now that I've seen it . . . I mean, I always believed you, but . . ."

"It's different seeing it yourself. I get it."

Ana nodded, her eyes wide. "Why is there a lizard creature? Or a fern creature, or a dog creature, or any of them? How can there still be menehune, living unseen all this time? It's just not possible. I get that it's magic, great, but magic has rules, doesn't it? How can a moʻo be a rock one moment and then climb up a waterfall the next? Where does that magic come from? In books, you know, like in *The Lion, the Witch and the Wardrobe*, you have to go through a door to get to the magic. Where's the door?"

"I don't know," I said helplessly. "I don't know anything more than you do, and I don't understand any of it. I don't think it's *possible* to understand. It all just . . . is."

Ana rested her chin on her knees and thought quietly. I let her think, let her try to puzzle it through, because finding answers was what Ana did. But I knew she wouldn't be able to find a logical explanation, not this time—because there was no door, no portal. There was just possible, and impossible, both existing at the same time.

CHAPTER TWELVE

MY AFTERNOON WITH ANA DID NOT, my mother assured me, suggest in any way that I was off the hook for the dangerously irresponsible behavior I had shown. "Not to mention the lying," she said sternly. "I'm still really upset about the lying."

I didn't bother trying to defend myself. I had lied, after all, and there was nothing I could say to explain any of it without being accused of more lying, which made talking at all feel pretty pointless. I acknowledged my wrongdoing and kept my head down, moving through the still-very-lengthy list of wedding chores without complaint.

I also wrote a letter to the Kaneshiros. It took me approximately fifty drafts and a not insignificant number of guilt-ridden tears, but it did eventually get written. My mother read it over, nodded in acknowledgment, and allowed me to bike over to post office to mail it.

What kind of stamp do you use for a letter like this? It's a silly thing to fuss over, I know, but I couldn't help it. Freedom flags? Mountain flora? Kittens?

I looked over the letter one last time before sealing it.

ALOHA, MR. AND MRS. KANESHIRO,

MY NAME IS EMMA ARRUDA, AND I'M WRITING TO YOU BECAUSE I KNEW YOUR SON WAS LOST AND I DIDN'T TELL ANYONE. I FOUND HIM IN THE WOODS EIGHT DAYS AGO NOW—SO ONLY ONE DAY AFTER HE WENT MISSING, THOUGH I DIDN'T KNOW THAT AT THE TIME. I BROUGHT HIM FOOD AND WATER AND A SLEEPING BAG, AND I KEPT HIM COMPANY AS MUCH AS I COULD. HE WAS VERY CONFUSED AT FIRST, BUT IT SEEMED TO ME LIKE HE WAS GETTING BETTER.

I DON'T KNOW HOW MUCH HE'S TOLD YOU ABOUT WHY HE WAS IN THE WOODS. I DON'T THINK THAT'S MY STORY TO TELL. BUT IT DOESN'T MATTER, ANYWAY—I SHOULD HAVE GOTTEN HIM HELP. I SHOULDN'T HAVE LEFT HIM THERE, AND I SHOULDN'T HAVE LEFT YOU FEELING SO SCARED FOR YOUR SON. I AM SO SORRY FOR THAT. I HOPE THAT HE IS OKAY, AND IF THERE IS ANYTHING I CAN DO TO HELP—WHETHER IT'S TO ANSWER ANY OF YOUR QUESTIONS, OR IF HE WANTS TO TALK TO ME FOR ANY REASON—PLEASE LET ME KNOW.

I REALLY AM SO VERY SORRY.

          E KALA MAI I'AU,
          EMMA

Sending the letter helped, but it wasn't quite enough to appease my parents—or my own sense of shame. Without being able to leave the house at night—or at all without permission—I had no way to contact Koa, much less to help the menehune. I hated it, and I worried constantly, but there wasn't anything I could do for them at the moment... and yet I itched to do *something*. It was Ana who suggested volunteering on Mauna Kea, helping with the Department of Land and Natural Resources' reforestation project.

Mauna Kea perfectly encapsulates the battle between sacred land and progress. Like all the mountains of Hawai'i, it is the remnant of a now-dormant shield volcano and the home of a number of Hawaiian deities, including Wākea, the sky father. Measured from the ocean floor, Mauna a Wākea is the tallest mountain on earth, and it is the piko— the navel, the connection between the spiritual and the physical—of the entire island chain.

It is also ideal for astronomy. Because of its high elevation, telescopes atop Mauna Kea are unusually free of atmospheric interference, allowing astronomers to observe distant objects with less distortion. It's also one of the darkest places on earth, being above the cloud layer and far from any urban centers. Some of the most significant astronomical discoveries have been made through the use of the telescopes that have been built at the summit, including exoplanets, galaxy clusters, gravitational waves, cosmology, and dark matter. I would always get a little burst of pride when I read about images of the Pillars of Creation being captured by the Subaru Telescope, or Keck finding the most distant known galaxy, or the James Clerk Maxwell Telescope recording the first-ever image of a supermassive black hole.

And yet, that's a lot of telescopes. And there are even more of them up there, now defunct and littering the summit, with nobody cleaning up the mess they made. The telescopes that are in use are also quite sensitive, and scientists there don't want the general public trooping around and, I don't know, breaking things, so access to the summit is limited. People are required to stay in designated areas, which aren't even particularly well marked, and so oftentimes someone will get yelled at and chased out without any understanding of what they've done wrong—and that has been known to include kanaka maoli who go up there to honor their ancestors through ceremonies and rituals that have been practiced for generations.

It all kind of came to a head with the proposal of the TMT, a thirty-meter telescope that would, if built, be one of the world's most advanced and powerful. It would also be enormous—thirty meters is pretty tall, after all—and while different suggestions were made to minimize its impact, it's hard to imagine how a telescope that big wouldn't dominate the summit, making it even more difficult to find the piko of the islands amid the rubble of technology. The environmental impact of the telescopes already in place has been harmful enough, as the fragile ecosystem of Mauna Kea, with its unique native species, is already crumbling. It would have been one thing if the Native Hawaiian community was ever consulted on the construction on any of these telescopes, or if there had been adequate provisions made for us to continue to live our lives and perform our sacred rites.

Not that I'd ever done anything like that. My mom was Catholic and my dad was an atheist, and that was pretty much the end of that in our family. And yet, meeting Koa and his people had changed things for me in a way that I couldn't really explain, and I found myself wanting to find a way to connect with that spiritual sense of place that I felt in the forest, as if maybe that was what was being honored and claimed by the people who went up the mauna to pray and chant.

Of course, that's not all people did up there. When it snowed, we brought boards up and rode down the slopes the same way we rode the waves—and sometimes we would even go to the beach after. Truck beds would be shoveled full of snow and driven back down to sea level, where melting snowmen would last for all of an hour or two. And that was important, too—it may not have been spiritual, but it was miraculous in its own way. How many places in the world can host both a snowball fight and a beach volleyball game, all in the same day?

These are things worth protecting, and a few years ago, thousands of protesters flocked to block the Mauna Kea access road, stopping construction on the TMT. The kia'i, or guardians, set up tents and wooden structures, creating a kind of village, where everyone had food to eat and work to do, whether it was teaching or building, repairing or learning. We didn't go to stay, but we did drive up there to donate food and warm clothing, and to listen. It went on for over a hundred days, with visits from activists and celebrities from all over the world—until it culminated in the arrest of several dozen kiaʻi, and eventually an agreement was reached to put construction of the TMT on hold.

And that's where it remained, leaving Mauna Kea in a limbo of questions. Who has the right to do what with this land? What is the impact of indigenous resistance? How do we honor cultural and spiritual significance as well as scientific study? It is, for now, at a stalemate.

Volunteering wasn't going to do much to fix any of that. But if we could go up there and plant some trees and weed out some invasives, it would feel like we were doing *something*, at least. Something that mattered.

Ana's dad, Peter, drove us. Ana and I sat together in the back seat of their old brick-red Suburban playing And Then, telling stories together, adding to plotlines that got increasingly bizarre with each passing mile. We turned off the highway and onto the narrow road to Waikiʻi, its swoops and dips making my stomach drop and then climb back up to my throat. We parked at the hunters' shed and got out to find a couple of guys waiting for us.

"I thought this was run by the Department of Land and Natural Resources?" I murmured to Ana. "Seems a little sketch. . . ."

"It is run by DLNR," Peter said, overhearing. "But really, it's a labor of love by these guys." Peter reached out to exchange manly clap-hugs before introducing us. "Lucas, Kaleo, this is my daughter, Ana, and her friend Emma."

"Howzit," Lucas said as we awkwardly shook hands. I never felt less adult than when I needed to shake hands with someone. "We're just waiting on a group from the Rotary Club, and then we'll get started."

The Rotary Club arrived in an entourage of SUVs, bankers and attorneys and realtors all piling out, slathered in sunscreen. Ana and I exchanged looks and made a silent vow to speak to them as little as was humanly possible.

"Okay," Lucas said. "Today we're going to be planting māmane and koa seedlings. I'm sure most of you know this already, but we'll just go over a bit of the history. Mauna Kea used to be a lot greener than it is today, but when it became ranchland, they planted kikuyu grass to feed the cattle." There was a chorus of moans, and I remembered my dad swearing at the tenacious, snakelike grass that grew like a vine across our lawn. Where kikuyu grows, not much else will—and the cattle wouldn't have helped matters, either. "So what we're trying to do," Lucas continued, "is bring back the native plants that originally grew here, restoring Mauna Kea's forest to its original state. So far, we've planted over twenty thousand trees . . . and today, we're going to plant another couple hundred."

Kaleo stepped forward. "Before we get started, though, I'm going to perform a chant, and then I'd like everyone to introduce themselves and tell us whom you are bringing with you to work today." I wrinkled my eyebrows at this, a little confused, and Kaleo smiled. "This chant is part of *Ka piko kaulana o ka 'aina*, a creation chant written by King Kamehameha III." He stood with his hands at his sides and faced the summit, chin held high. He paused for a moment, and then inhaled. He called:

TRANSLATION:

Mālie 'ikea ka moku me ka honua	Serenely visible are island and earth,
Pa'a ia lewa lani i ka lima 'ākau o Wākea	Held firmly in heavenly space by the right hand of Wākea
'O ka moku lā ho'i	That shall be an island
Ko luna, 'o wai lā?	Who shall be above—who?
'O ke ao, 'o ia ho'i hā	The cloud, that is who it shall be
'O ke ao ho'i hā ko luna nei	A cloud shall be up here
'O wai lā auane'i ko lalo lā?	Who shall be below?
'O ka mauna, 'o ia ho'i hā	The mountain, that is who it shall be
Ua hānau ka mauna a Wākea	Born was the mountain of Wākea

There was silence when he finished, save for the bubbly warble of a pālila singing in the brush. Kaleo said, "Okay, thanks everyone. Today, I am bringing my nephew. He's four years old, and I want him to grow up in a world where there are a lot more trees."

And so it went, around the circle, with each Rotary Club member offering their own reason for being there. I bit my lip as my turn grew closer—I was very clear on whom I was doing this for, but I couldn't exactly say menehune.

In the end, what I said was this: "I'm Emma, and today I'm bringing someone I failed. I can't help him, and so I'm doing this. It's . . ." My throat closed up, and Ana's sympathetic face blurred as my eyes watered. "It's not enough. But here I am."

Ana reached out and squeezed my hand. "I'm Ana," she said steadily. "And today I'm bringing the hope that we can make a difference."

Peter went last, and after he'd introduced himself, he said, "I'm bringing with me two young women who will change the world."

Lucas laughed at him, breaking the tension. "You're not supposed to say people who are actually here! But I guess that'll do," he said with a wink at me. "All right, everybody back in your cars and follow me—we'll be heading up the road a couple of miles."

Ana and I were quiet as we joined the caravan driving up the dusty road. When at last we stopped, Lucas and Kaleo opened the back of their truck to reveal rows of stacked trays of seedlings, all packed in slim plastic containers shaped like champagne flutes, wet and dripping with dirt-stained water.

Lucas pulled out a portable hole digger and moved along methodically, creating row after row of holes that we all then filled, carefully easing the māmane or koa seedlings out of their containers and packing them gently into the earth, sealing them with whatever mulch we could find in the surrounding dry grasses, trying to keep the moisture in. In one clump I found a small yellow-gray feather. It might well have belonged to the yellow finches that overran the island, but as I slid it into my pocket, I chose to believe it belonged to the pālila, the critically endangered honeycreeper that lived only on the upper slopes of Mauna Kea.

We worked for hours and hours, moving back and forth between the truck and the hillside, lifting and kneeling, planting and tending, in high elevation with low oxygen and without even a hint of shade. It was, if I'm being honest, downright miserable—but not a single person complained. Everyone just worked away, in gentle camaraderie, pausing occasionally to take in the view—which was absolutely worth taking in. From where we stood, on the tallest mountain, we could see four others—Hualālai, standing green and just a bit jagged, like a cupped hand held over the earth. Mauna Loa, with its startlingly gentle slope, arching long and smooth like an ocean swell. In the distance, the small lump of Kīlauea, coughing out smoke as the lava bubbled on the crater floor. And finally, across the sea, the majesty of Haleakalā, the place where the demigod Maui wrestled the sun from the sky, slowing its journey and lengthening our days.

This particular day felt more than long enough, but at the end of it, as we posed for a group photo and exchanged happy but tired waves goodbye, Peter asked if Ana and I had enough energy left in us to go for a quick hike.

Ana groaned. "Dad, no—what? We've been working *all day*. I'm hot and dirty, and I want a boba tea. I do not want a hike."

"All right, if you say so," Peter said with a shrug. "I just thought, since we're out here, we could run up to the summit and go see Lake Waiau."

Ana and I exchanged a look. Lake Waiau is a freshwater lake, a rarity in the islands, as most bodies of water are either coastal or brackish—but Lake Waiau is fed entirely by rainwater and snowmelt. It is the highest-elevation lake in the islands, and at thirteen thousand feet, it's the third-highest alpine lake in the world. It had supposedly been created when the cinder cone that had once spouted lava atop Mauna Kea settled into a bowl and the glaciers formed during various ice ages somehow transmuted the earth beneath, turning it into clay so that it could hold water. With the porosity of the rock, the lake really ought to have drained by now, but it hasn't. Its depth can vary, but it is always there, and so it remains something of a geological mystery.

A mystery which neither of us had ever visited. I went up to Mauna Kea only to play in the snow or look at the stars, and neither activity was particularly conducive to hanging by a lake.

"Okay," Ana said at last. "But boba teas after."

We turned onto the winding road that led up to the summit. At the base of this road stood the remains of shelters that had housed the kia'i during the protests. The stone ahu they had built stood tall and sturdy, draped with fading lei and tī leaves. We drove past rusting Quonset huts and waving brown grasses, my nose beginning to ache as we climbed. There were plenty of signs indicating that altitude sickness can be lethal, and so we obeyed their instructions and paused at 9,200 feet, resting at the visitor center for the suggested half hour, giving our bodies time to adjust.

Peter handed us each one of the sweatshirts he kept stored in the back of the car (Big Island weather being eternally variable), and Ana and I set off to explore. We bought some overpriced astronaut ice cream (there was an unspoken understanding that consuming anything an astronaut would eat brought us closer to the stars) and laughed at the sign that read:

BEWARE OF INVISIBLE COWS!
DARK-COLORED COWS ARE OFTEN INVISIBLE
IN DARKNESS AND/OR IN FOG.
USE EXTREME CAUTION!

It seemed the feral ghost cows of Volcano had also made their way to the slopes of Mauna Kea. Ana wandered off to read about the telescopes (all thirteen of them) while I read about some of the legends that surrounded Mauna Kea. The Hawaiian pantheon includes kupua, beings of supernatural powers who can take a variety of kinolau, including natural manifestations like boars, fish, rain, and even locations. Wākea's kinolau is the entirety of Mauna Kea, but I didn't expect to be reading about Pele up here—and yet, of course she was here. Mauna Kea is a volcano, after all.

In the tradition of most storytelling that explains natural phenomena—Greek mythology and Norse legends, for instance—the kupua of Hawaiʻi behave entirely irrationally, like spoiled children. And like children, Poliʻahu, the goddess of snow and the summit of Mauna Kea, and her sisters Waiau and Lilinoe went holua sledding. They were competitive, racing down and scrambling back up to go again, sliding all the way from the top of the mountain to Laupahoehoe on the Hāmākua Coast.

A stranger approached them and asked if she could join their game. She introduced herself as Keahilele, or the leaping flame. Poliʻahu and her sisters agreed, and Keahilele lived up to her name—she shot down the mountain so fast she left sparks in her wake. But Poliʻahu could call upon the ice, and when they reached the end, she was declared the winner.

Keahilele stamped her feet in fury, and the ground beneath them shook, cracking open as smoke poured from the earth below. Poliʻahu and her sisters fled, knowing now that they had been duped—this was Pele, known for her rages and her fiery vengeance. Pele cried after them, vowing to destroy the mountain that held them. When Poliʻahu reached the summit, she cloaked herself in snow, creating a blanket of white protection.

It wasn't enough. The summit began to erupt, and below Lake Waiau, cracks appeared as more eruptions began, a chain of fountaining lava that moved down the slope they had slid down in their game. The lava melted the snow, but

Poliʻahu called upon her sisters, and Lilinoe and Waiau brought down the mist and the rain, blinding Pele. Poliʻahu took advantage of her distraction, packing the snow and water into ice. The ice slid down, pressing, freezing the lava beneath it until all that remained was hard black rock. Pele retreated to Kīlauea, where she remains to this day.

The odd thing about this story was how eerily accurate it was, from a scientific perspective. The Laupahoehoe volcanic series occurred during the same period as the Makanaka glacial episode on the summit of Mauna Kea, and the glaciers that sealed in the lava formed a hardened rock that is now known as hawaiite. Geologists couldn't explain the sledding part, though.

Ana tapped my shoulder and cocked her head toward the car. "You ready to go?"

We drove up past the astronomer dormitories and through the mist—through Lilinoe, I thought absently—until we were above the cloud layer, the car roaring as we climbed the twisting gravel road. The parking lot was empty save for a place to scrape your boots, to clear them of the fungus that was damaging the ʻōhiʻa—not that there were trees up here. There was nothing but rock, the Puʻu Waiau cinder cone stretching up toward the gray-blue sky.

It was quite a bit colder up here than it had been at the visitor center, and at first Ana and I walked quickly to try to get warm, but soon enough it became clear that speed was not really available to us. The hike was neither hard nor long, but at just over thirteen thousand feet, the altitude made it difficult to breathe. I took deep, steadying breaths through my mouth and focused on putting one foot in front of the other. Peter kept offering us water, insisting that hydration was key.

It was an odd thing. Even though I knew I was walking to a lake—that was the purpose of the trip, after all—I was still surprised when I saw it. We crested a hill and there it was, nestled in the basin of the puʻu like a bowl of water. It was just so unexpected, to see signs of life in such a barren place, the water gently lapping at the grassy shore in the breeze, the winds quieter here, sheltered.

Peter and Ana started to walk forward, but I held out a hand to stop them. I thought of Kaleo, chanting before we set to work planting trees. I didn't know that chant; I didn't speak ʻŌlelo beyond a few words here and there, and I felt, as I so often did, like I didn't know enough about Hawaiʻi—that I wasn't *Hawaiian enough*.

But I also thought of Hilo, and how he'd fought so hard with Koa to preserve a forest that wasn't even his—it was mine, and I had done nothing for it. I wondered what he would think of me, standing here now and offering nothing to the lake in exchange for its blessing.

Because the truth was I did know one chant. I'd learned it last year during Hawaiian history class. It wasn't really appropriate for this moment—it was sung by Pele's sister Hiʻiaka when she asked permission to ford a river on Kauaʻi—but I thought that just maybe, if my intentions were right, then perhaps it wouldn't matter if the words weren't exactly suited to the moment. I took off my sweatshirt despite the chill in the air, and my skin rose in goose bumps. I kept my arms by my sides and gazed down at the still waters of Waiau.

TRANSLATION:

Kūnihi ka mauna i ka laʻi e	*Steep stands the mountain*
O Waiʻaleʻale la i Wailua	*in calm*
Huki aʻela i ka lani	*Profile of Waiʻaleʻale*
Ka papa ʻauwai o Kawaikini	*at Wailua*
Ālai ʻia aʻe la e Nounou	*Drawn away into the heavens*
Nalo Kaipuhaʻa	*Is the riverbed course*
Ka laulā mauka o Kapaʻa, e	*of Kawaikini*
Mai paʻa i ka leo	*Blocked off by Nounou*
He ʻole kāhea mai, e	*Hidden is the valley*
	of Kaipuhaʻa
	The broad expanse upland
	of Kapaʻa
	Give voice and make answer
	No calling voice in reply

Ana and Peter watched in silence. When I finished, I looked to the sky, to the water. Had permission been granted? There was no voice, no light shining from the heavens, nothing to indicate yes or no. And yet, I didn't feel we were *unwelcome*. There was a sense of calm expectation and when I released a breath, Ana, Peter, and I moved quietly down to the shore. As we walked, Ana reached out and took my hand, squeezing it gently.

There was an ahu at the water's edge, though it wasn't as carefully constructed as the one at the foot of the mountain. On it were the remains of offerings, including bits of fruit, shells, and scattered flowers. I searched in my pockets for something to leave and found the yellow feather. I held it to my heart for a moment, then tucked it carefully between the rocks so it wouldn't blow away.

"You know," Peter said conversationally. "There's a story about birds and Lake Waiau. Apparently, one of her forms is a bird that can be heard calling high up on the slopes—higher than the pālila can survive, colder than any bird could withstand. Some say its chirp is nothing more than the cracking of the ice in winter," he finished, shrugging.

"Well, it's not winter now," Ana said, ever practical. "The lake isn't even frozen."

It was true. As cold as it was, it was well above freezing, and there was no sign of snow or ice anywhere. I knelt and trailed my fingers into the water. The ache of its chill was startling but also comforting, as if its frigid stillness could cleanse me somehow.

I cupped my hands and held the water to my lips, blowing on it. "Forgive me," I whispered. "I know I did the wrong thing. I know I haven't fixed anything. Help me understand what to do."

Of course, there was no answer. There was only the crunch of the rocks beneath Ana's feet and the absent-minded humming coming from Peter as he peered into the grasses that grew along the lakeside. The water rippled gently, the gray blue of its shallow depths reflecting the gray blue of the endless sky. And in the distance, I thought I could hear the call of an unknown bird.

CHAPTER THIRTEEN

THERE WAS NO WAY I COULD SNEAK OUT at night, not again. But maybe I could find a way to talk to Koa somehow, even in daylight. So the next morning, I went back to the construction site. Hilo's dad was there—I recognized him seated atop the backhoe, which was clearly back in good working order. They'd cleared all the way to where Hilo had been sleeping, and his makeshift house was gone. At least they were moving away from the menehune's lava tube, though I knew that couldn't last forever.

I'd brought Mālie up with me (so of course Snookie was hanging around, too). I focused on the feel of my fingers in her fur and tried not to panic while I waited for Hilo's dad to go on break.

Finally, he climbed down from the backhoe and went over to the cooler to get some water. Mālie wouldn't go anywhere if Snookie didn't, so I left her there and walked around the edge of the site until I stood in front of him.

"Excuse me, Mr. Kaneshiro?"

He swallowed his water and looked at me.

"I'm . . . um, my name is Emma? I wrote you a letter?"

His expression shifted in a way I couldn't quite read. "You're Alika's girl."

I felt my face grow hot. "Oh no. I mean we're not . . ."

"I mean, the girl he's been talking about. I think. He hasn't been making that much sense," he said.

My heart sank. I had sort of been hoping that being out of the forest meant that Hilo had gotten all better somehow. "Is he okay?" I asked hesitantly.

Mr. Kaneshiro shrugged. "He's getting better and making more sense every day. He told us you'd been taking care of him." He looked at me sideways.

I swallowed hard. "I mean, I guess, but I shouldn't have . . ." I took a deep breath. "I'm so sorry. I should have told someone where he was. He could have gotten so badly hurt, and you must have been so scared. I'm really, really sorry."

Mr. Kaneshiro just stood there looking at me for a moment, and then he nodded, his face softening. "I appreciate it. I don't understand it, but Alika says you couldn't have told anyone. And I trust my boy." He took another gulp of water. "That your dog over there?"

"Mālie, the whippet, is. The other one just kind of lives all over."

"Good-looking dog. Good hunters, whippets."

I could tell he was trying to be nice. "Yeah, she's a good dog," I said.

Kainoa, the manager guy, hollered over to Mr. Kaneshiro. "Isaac! Back to work!"

Mr. Kaneshiro waved an arm at him, as if to say, *In a minute*. He squinted at me. "Alika also says we can't cut down the forest. He's been begging me to stop it."

I answered carefully, not sure how much he'd been told—or how much he believed. "It would certainly be a lot better if it didn't happen," I said.

He sighed and rubbed the back of his neck. "Look, I hate this job," he said abruptly. "Kainoa is a pain in the ass, and I don't like clear-cutting native forest. Nobody does. But I need work. And this is my job, you know? I've got to put food on the table."

"You don't owe me an explanation," I said softly. He didn't owe me anything at all.

"No, but Alika doesn't understand, or he refuses to. He can barely look at me."

Kainoa yelled again, and Mr. Kaneshiro sighed. "I've got to go."

"Will you say hi to Hilo . . . I mean, to Alika for me?"

He nodded, took one last gulp of water, and climbed into his backhoe.

After waving goodbye to Mr. Kaneshiro, I headed back to where my bike was parked alongside the road . . . but then I backtracked into the woods, Mālie and Snookie on my heels. At first, I wasn't sure if I could even find my way back to the lava tube where the menehune were living. But it turned out to be easy, almost as if the trees were parting, the ferns moving aside, guiding me. An 'apapane flew ahead of me, its bright red wings flashing, and as long as I followed it, I didn't feel lost.

When I found the entrance to the tunnel, it appeared empty. There was no sign that anyone lived there, much less an entire community. I crept in, feeling like I was trespassing. "Hello?" I whispered.

As I moved farther into the tunnel, it quickly became pitch black, despite the sun shining outside, and with no menehune to guide me, I couldn't see a thing. I felt my way along, one hand touching the wall and the other waving blindly in front of me, hoping to avoid smacking my head on a low part of the ceiling. I put one foot carefully in front of the other, brushing it back and forth to assure myself I wouldn't trip. I must have been moving slower than a snail.

"Koa?" I whisper-called. "I'm sorry to bother you, but I thought you'd want to know what's going on?"

My hand brushed something soft, and I jumped back with a squeak, my heart thumping wildly.

"Shh," the soft thing whispered. "You'll wake everyone up."

I tried to get my breathing back under control as my eyes immediately began to adjust to being in the presence of a menehune. The darkness faded away, until I could see a young, strong woman standing in front of me. Her arms were crossed in front of her chest, and her hair was pulled back in a knot at the base of her neck.

"Hi," I whispered. "I'm Emma."

She sighed. "I know who you are."

"Can I come in? Can I talk to Koa? It's important."

She paused, thinking. "I'll go get him," she said at last. "You'll just wake everyone up, and then the keiki will be exhausted all day. Wait here."

As she walked away, the darkness fell again, and I tried not to panic. I had never been claustrophobic, and I'd been in plenty of lava tubes before—including this one, of course. But knowing that she was moving away from me, so softly that I couldn't even hear it, leaving me all alone in the black with no sense of time or space? It wasn't my favorite experience.

The moments seemed to drag on forever, though I knew it couldn't really have been that long. At last, Koa's voice sounded near me, and I jumped and squeaked again. I hadn't even heard him approach.

"Thank you, Alamea," he said. "You can rest now. I'll stand guard the rest of the day."

I didn't hear her leave.

"What is it, Emma?" Koa said, sounding tired. But as my eyes adjusted and I looked closer, I saw that he wasn't sleepy tired—he was exhausted from too much worry and too little hope.

"Alika—Hilo, the boy—had to go home. I tried, before he left, to halt the construction, but it's moving forward.

They're going to be digging right above here any day now. Koa, you have to get your people out. I know this is your home, but it's just not safe. We can find somewhere for you to go. There are other lava tubes, other safe places—"

"It's not about that," he said flatly. "We cannot leave."

I wanted to tear my hair out in frustration. "You can go in the nighttime! I've seen you all outside; I know you can. I'll help you figure out how to, I don't know, be sneaky! We'll move slowly—no one will find you! I know it's a risk, but if you stay here, you will all *die*, Koa."

He sighed heavily. "I know. But Emma, you don't understand. It's our kuleana. We have no choice. We must stay."

"You're right," I said, my eyes filling with tears. "I don't understand."

He reached up and laid a hand on my shoulder, squeezing gently. "Come tonight," he said. "I will show you, and you will understand."

"Absolutely not," my mom said.

"Please," I begged again. "I need to go. It won't be for long, just for an hour or so. It's safe; I promise."

"It's not just about safety," my dad said. "It's about trust."

"But that's why I'm asking you instead of sneaking out!" My voice rose in frustration. "I'm very sorry I lied to you, I absolutely should not have done that, but this is important. People are counting on me."

"What people?" my mom asked. "Who is counting on you?"

I hesitated, knowing what the response would be, but there wasn't any other truthful answer I could give. "Menehune," I said at last.

"Emma, come on, give us a break," my dad said, rolling his eyes. "If you're going to lie to us, at least try to make it believable."

"But that's how you know I'm not lying! I *know* how it sounds, but it's real. Why can't you believe me?"

There was a long pause, and my dad looked to my mother. She spread her hands, and he shrugged. "Emma, menehune are stories," he said. "You are old enough to know better than this."

"*No*, Dad, they're not—"

"But," he said, ignoring me, "even if I don't agree with everything you're saying, I understand that this is important to you. Here's what we can do. You may not go riding off on your bike at night. That is not safe, end of story. But I can drive you up there and go with you to do whatever it is you feel you need to do. Deal?"

I hesitated. I'd been invited, but my dad hadn't. I didn't know how Koa would feel about me bringing him, but I didn't exactly have a choice. "Can I have some privacy when we're up there? I'll stay where you can see me," I added quickly.

Mom and Dad shared another glance. "All right," he said. "I can do that. But hurry up. I want to get this over with and get back home."

I didn't need to be told twice. I ran to my room to pull on my sweatshirt and sneakers, while Dad sat down heavily on the steps and tugged on his boots. "Don't you want a flashlight?" he asked.

"I won't need one," I told him, and he shrugged.

We didn't say much on the short ride up Wright Road. It was a clear night, the Milky Way like spilled paint overhead, and there were lights that hung in the sky like UFOs in the distance—they were cars driving up to the summit of Mauna Kea, presumably to stargaze.

Dad pulled over on the side of the road and climbed out of the car.

"Can you wait here?" I asked. "I'll just be a minute."

Dad nodded, and I ran across the cleared field, to where I knew Koa would be waiting. He stood at the edge of the trees, shadowed so that my father couldn't see him.

"I'm sorry," I said, gesturing back at my dad. "I wasn't allowed to come by myself."

Koa gave a short nod. "That's all right," he said. "Come, I have to show you something."

"But my dad," I said. "I can't go with you. I have to stay where he can see me."

Koa shrugged. "Then he will see you." He gestured to his side, and a hāpuʻu fern bent itself toward him. "Come," Koa said again.

I looked at the fern, and in the space between blinks it shifted, until it looked like me. Well, not really, but it looked roughly my size and shape, so that from where my father was waiting by the car, he would see the fern, and his mind would tell him he was seeing me.

"I, um, all right." I was pretty sure this counted as more lying, but I couldn't think what else to do. I had a fern impersonator. This was not a circumstance with which I'd had much experience. I followed Koa into the forest. He always moved quickly, but tonight he was swift, so swift that even though the trees and branches moved aside for me it was difficult to keep up. We ran past the entrance to his lava-tube home, and then, just there, not even very far from the clearing we'd left behind, was a heiau.

I couldn't believe I'd never seen it before. Unlike the cave entrance, it wasn't hidden. It was just surrounded by forest, with no paths leading to or from it that I could see. "How did no one know this was here?" I whispered. "Wouldn't they have had to do an archaeological survey before starting construction?"

"We hid it," Koa said simply. "We have always kept hidden."

The stone temple was small and simple, lava rocks forming a raised platform with low walls surrounding the sides. There was a raised ahu or altar at one end, much like the one I'd seen on Mauna Kea, and the menehune had placed offerings there. Koa approached the ahu and placed his hands upon it, bowing his head. I bowed in turn. The forest pressed in on us, dropping spores from the ferns and leaves from the trees around the edges of the heiau. But it didn't feel disrespectful. The heiau was clearly well cared for, nurtured as if it were a living thing. The forest that encroached was not dismantling the heiau—it was participating in it. It was a part of it.

"This is yours to tend?" I asked, my voice low. "This heiau is your kuleana?"

Koa nodded.

"Is it . . . is it sacred to Kū?" I asked, hesitant. Kū was the ancient Hawaiian god of war, and many heiau were dedicated to him. But that didn't really seem to track with the flavor of reverence I sensed from Koa and his people.

Koa scoffed. "Of course not. Not to any of the gods, even Pele. With all due respect," he added, bowing his head in the direction of Kīlauea crater, where our fire goddess dwelled. No one mocked Pele, not ever. "It's a menehune heiau. It's sacred to the forest."

"This forest, specifically?"

Koa shook his head. "No." He frowned, trying to think. "Sacred to . . . to nature. To tending. To mālama. Does that make sense to you?"

It did. I honestly couldn't think of anything *more* sacred than the act of caring for and honoring the 'āina, the land and all that it held.

"We cannot leave this heiau," Koa said, regretful but unwavering. "It is ours, and there is no one else. If we do not care for it, the fungus that is eating our 'ōhi'a will spread, the rain will dry up, the birds will be silenced, and the forest will die. There is no choice."

I thought about the arid slopes of Mauna Kea, the summit littered with the remains of abandoned telescopes. I thought about the dry dirt of Lāhainā, the original seat of the Hawaiian Kingdom, which had once been a wetland until the sugarcane drained it of nutrients so that only dried grasses would grow, grasses that caught in a wildfire so hot that the bones of the people who lived there melted into the barren earth.

"I understand," I said, tears making my eyes blur. I reached out to touch the ahu and bowed my head. "I'm so sorry."

CHAPTER FOURTEEN

I SAID VERY LITTLE THAT NIGHT. MY PARENTS exchanged a Look when my dad and I got home, and whatever the look said, it was enough that they left me alone. Which was good, because I had no idea what I would tell them.

With nothing else to do the next morning, I threw myself into wedding prep, which by that point meant laying paving stones as a pathway from the backyard to the house so people wouldn't slip in the mud if they had to go to the bathroom. Even though it was an outdoor wedding, Puʻulena wanted an aisle for her and Naomi to walk down. Not a red carpet or anything, but shells from the beaches in California that Naomi went to when she was growing up. (It did seem only fair to have *something* Naomi-centric, given that they were flying out here to Puʻulena's home to get married.) They'd shipped us a box, so after laying the paving stones, I crawled around the lawn arranging the shells just so, composing an aisle leading up from the base of the hill where they would get married.

Our work was no longer being undone by the menehune, but I almost wished it were, because I knew that this meant that Koa had given up on any help from me—as well he should have. I was literally helpless—I had nothing to offer the menehune, even after they had trusted me enough to ask for my aid. It was a horrible feeling.

I found myself missing Hilo. It was a strange thing, really—I hardly knew him to begin with, and I had no idea what he would be like now that the 'ōhi'a tree had released him from its curse. Maybe he would go back to being the way he'd been when we first met, all cool and arrogant. Not anyone who would ever want to hang out with someone like me.

Somehow, I couldn't really believe that would be the case. Somehow, I felt like I *knew* Hilo, the person he was when nobody was watching. And I felt like he knew me, too—as if we were the only two people who truly understood what was happening in these forests. The only two people who knew how much it mattered.

The next day was Wednesday. Dad had taken off the rest of the week in preparation for the wedding, and I had assumed we would be, I don't know, digging up our mossy lawn and replacing it with sod or something. But I woke up to the thud of beach towels being tossed down the stairs.

"We go beach!" my dad yelled.

There were plenty of people in Hawai'i who went to the beach every day. We were not those people. Living up on the mountain where we did, it was a bit of a trek to get to where the good beaches were—two hours away on the other side of the island. So when we decided to go to the beach, we made it worthwhile, bringing a cooler and beach chairs and snorkels and masks and bodyboards and all the things. We would stop for sushi and chips at the grocery store on the way and make an entire day of it.

"What, do we need to go to Costco or something?" I poured myself a bowl of Cheerios as my mom gulped down her coffee. The wholesale store wasn't far from the beach, and shipping prices being what they were, everybody on the island tended to buy in bulk.

"Yes," she admitted. "We need wine and vodka, and your dad wants to make haupia for the wedding."

I raised an eyebrow. "That's going to be a lot of haupia."

She rolled her eyes. "I know. But you know your father...."

It's true. There was no talking Dad out of something he'd decided he wanted to do.

"It's not just about the Costco trip," Dad said, coming into the kitchen. "You girls have been working too hard. We need a break. So we go beach!"

He always loved saying that.

I went to go change into my swimsuit and threw a T-shirt and shorts over the top. I helped load up the car and then climbed into the back seat.

We hit traffic before we even made it to Hilo. "What is going on?" My dad angled his head to try to see what was causing the congestion. "It's the middle of the day; it can't be rush hour."

My mom calmly pulled out her phone to look it up. "Oh, wow," she said. "It's construction. They're working to repair the damage done in Leilani Estates during the flow."

"But that's like fifteen miles away!"

"Okay, so there's a backup." She shrugged. "I'm sure it'll clear out soon. Anyway, it took them long enough to get started on it."

I looked down the road, though we were much too far away for me to be able to see anything. Back toward home, Kīlauea still simmered, the lava bubbling and frothing gently in the crater, like a pot of thick soup. It was always present, always a source of awe and disastrous potential, every so often shaking with an earthquake or coughing out a burp of fountaining lava. You got used to it.

The traffic jam eventually cleared up, and we drove on. Unfortunately, after an hour or so of reading in the car, my motion sickness kicked in, just as it always did. I put my book away and stared out the window, watching the green slopes of the Hāmākua Coast shift into the arid grasslands of Kawaihae.

It was crowded at Hāpuna Beach by the time we got there, so we had to park at the top lot and walk down. My dad was grumbling because it was summer and that meant there were no good waves, so therefore he'd be bored in about fifteen minutes—if that—but since neither my mom nor I surfed, we didn't mind. Small waves meant better snorkeling.

I kicked off my slippers even though the white sand was scorching hot and burned my feet. I hated walking in the sand in slippers. We set up chairs and slathered on the sunscreen, and as soon as mine was dry I dashed into the water. The lapping waves cooled my feet, and I wriggled my toes down into the fine sand. A towheaded toddler in a swim diaper ran along the water toward me, until a wave knocked her down. I picked her up and set her back on her feet as her mom came running over.

"Oh, sweetie, are you okay?" She squeezed her daughter, who was more interested in licking the salt water off her arms. "Thank you," the woman said to me. "I think I must have dozed off. We just got in yesterday and I'm *so jet-lagged*."

"It's all good," I said. "She was fine."

"Are you here with your family? Where are you in from?"

I shrugged. "I'm from here, actually."

The woman gasped and turned to yell up the beach to her husband. "Honey! She's a *native*!"

I widened my eyes at her and felt my face turning red. "Okay, I hope you have a nice visit," I said, and turned to walk away.

"You're so lucky to live here," she called after me. "It's so beautiful. But, like, there aren't as many flowers as I would have thought?"

I wasn't sure how to reply to that. "Um, maybe you'll find some flowers on the Hilo side? And they usually have plumeria and hibiscus at the hotels."

"I meant, like, wildflowers, like growing on the side of the highway."

I shrugged again. This side of the island, where the best beaches are, is pretty much just lava rock and dry grassland. Not much grows on lava. I edged away. "I'm just going to . . . I think I hear my mom calling me. Have a nice time. . . ."

I fled back to my parents. My mom had cracked open her book, and my dad was already looking restless. I suggested to him that we swim around to the small inlet over on the other side of the beach past the area sectioned off for the hotel, and I think he agreed mainly because it was something to do. Hāpuna was by no means a big beach by typical Hawai'i standards—Waikīkī Beach on O'ahu was two miles long, while Hāpuna was a measly half mile—and yet, for the Big Island, that was a lot. Our shores tended to be rockier, what with being newly formed by lava, geologically speaking.

So rather than swimming all that way, we walked the length of the beach, our feet sinking into the sand with every wave that crashed around our ankles, avoiding thrown Frisbees and kids riding the gentle surf. We rounded the rocky outcropping that sort of separated the "hotel beach" from the hoi polloi and briefly discussed sneaking in to go jump in the pool before deciding that if we got caught my mom would be absolutely furious with us.

Instead, we went ahead with our original plan, pulling on our masks and snorkels before wading out into the waves until it was deep enough to swim. I wasn't as strong a swimmer as my dad or my sister. She'd played water polo, so she was a badass. My parents had made me join the YWCA swim team last year because apparently sport is good for . . . something. It was unclear what.

That said, even if I wasn't fast, I could stay afloat and keep going for a long while. I watched the ripples of the sand along the ocean floor as we swam, the fish moving below us. I could hear uhu chomping at the coral, and a couple of yellow tangs swam in and out of the reef.

By the time we made it to the little beach—and this one really was little, just a tiny patch of sand that disappeared with the high tide—I was out of breath. I tore off my mask and dipped my face into the cool, clear water. We hung out in the shallows for a little bit, but to be honest, there wasn't much to do, so before too long, we simply swam back and then retraced our steps along the sand.

Dad flopped down onto his chair and opened his sushi. But even after the long swim, I still felt . . . on edge. I needed to be doing something. I shook my head when Mom offered me lunch. "I'm going to go jump off the rock," I told her.

She made a face. "Really, Emma?"

"It's fine, Mom," I said, rolling my eyes. "I've done it hundreds of times."

"I know, just . . . be careful, okay?"

"I will." I dropped a kiss onto the top of her head and walked up the beach, breaking into a run when the sand got too hot on my feet. I stopped to pluck a leaf from the naupaka kahakai that grew along the rock wall at the back of the beach. Letting my feet rest in the shade of bushes, I ran a finger along the tiny petals of the white half flower. It wasn't really identical to the naupaka kuahiwi—the size was different, as were the number of petals. And yet it was odd, the way two such vastly different plants, growing in such opposing climates, had evolved to produce two such strangely shaped and eerily similar blossoms.

I thought about what Hilo—Alika, I reminded myself— had said that day, sitting outside my driveway. *Two worlds*, he'd said. *Always separate now.* I wondered if some version of the legend was true—if there had been a time when that which was separate had once been whole. I couldn't help but wish, as I always did when I looked at the naupaka, that there was some way that these two half flowers could be put back together.

I gripped the waxy naupaka leaf in my hand as I ran back toward the shore, letting out a breath of relief when the waves cooled my feet. I jumped into the water and swam for the rocks. The shoreline was crowded as always, but once I swam past the break, it cleared out. There was a selection of rocks to choose from, but I had my favorite—it had a relatively easy climb, and the sharp edges of the lava had been worn smooth enough by the waves that they wouldn't scrape my hands and feet, but not so smooth that they were slippery with algae. I timed my climb with a wave, allowing the water to boost me up the first hurdle, helping me find my grip. I scrambled up until I found the spot to jump—high enough to be worthwhile and straight enough that I would plunge over sand and not rock.

It's not considered particularly cool to hold your nose when jumping into the water. Then again, it's even less cool to come up snorting and choking because water inevitably went up your nose because you *didn't* hold it. My dad had taught me a trick his mom had taught him— to hold a leaf in your mouth so, when you jumped, the force of the water would push the leaf up against your nose, sealing it safely and stylishly closed. I bit down on the naupaka leaf, waited for a wave to come, and jumped into its embrace. The leaf brushed up against my face as I sank into the clear blue water, until I opened my mouth, releasing it to the sea. When I came up for air, I didn't pause. I swam out toward the horizon, and I kept swimming until there was no one in front of me or beside me, until so long as I faced out to sea, I couldn't see or hear anyone but myself. I took a deep breath and blew out as much air as I could, dropping down to the bottom. When I felt my feet touch the sand, I looked up. The surface wasn't far away, maybe only a few feet, but it looked impossible, even with my vision blurred underwater.

How did we exist in a world that was mostly water, an element that we couldn't survive in? And how could the menehune exist in a world that was destroying their home, and destroying itself?

My lungs were desperate for air, but I didn't want to surface yet. My eyes blurred even more as they filled with tears, the salt water from my body mixing with the salt water of the ocean.

At last, my body reacted without me, pushing up to the surface, and I gasped in a huge breath of air.

And in that moment, that burst of oxygen, I remembered something.

CHAPTER FIFTEEN

I SCRAMBLED OUT OF THE WATER, STILL PANTING, and flopped down onto the sand next to my parents.

"Dad," I said. "Tell me the story of Laka and the canoe."

My dad squinted at me. "Laka? Why? You know that story. Everyone knows that story."

"Please. I need to hear it again."

"Eat some lunch," Mom said, passing me the sushi. I rolled my eyes, but I accepted it, cracking open the bento box and taking a swig of iced tea.

My dad shrugged and began. "Laka went to the forest to find a tree so he could build a canoe. His village was down at the shore, so it was a long walk up through the ahupuaʻa until he reached the forest. He looked around for a long time, trying to find a tree that was tall and straight and strong, and large enough to hold his weight and stay afloat. At last, he found the perfect koa tree, and so he set to work bringing it down. It took him all day, chopping at it with his stone tool, but at last the tree fell. He bowed to it, offering his thanks, and then headed home, exhausted from the day's work. He would come back to begin carving it tomorrow.

"But when he returned the next morning, there was the tree—back upright and growing, as if he had never cut it down. He thought he must have dreamed the whole thing, so he went to work again, chopping away at it, until the tree fell. Once again, he was exhausted, and so once again he went home. But—you guessed it—when he came back the next day, there the tree was again, standing just as if he'd never touched it.

"Well, Laka wasn't having any more of that. So he chopped down the tree again, but this time, instead of going home, he hid. And he waited, and he waited until the sun went down.

"He had just started to doze off when he heard voices. He peered through the underbrush, careful not to make any noise, and then he saw them—a group of menehune, getting set to hoist the tree back up. With a shout, Laka ran out from his hiding place and snatched one of them, grabbing him by the shoulders. 'What are you doing?' he demanded. 'Don't you know you're wasting all my hard work?'

"The menehune he had caught kicked him in the shins. 'Your hard work for what?' he said. 'You don't even know *how* to shape a canoe.'

"And this, sadly, was true. Laka did not know how to shape a canoe. The kupuna who knew how to kālai waʻa had died without teaching anyone, and no one in the village knew how. This was why it was so important for Laka to make this canoe, for without someone to build canoes, how would they travel to the other islands? How would they fish? How would they feed the village?

"Laka sighed and let the menehune go. 'You're right,' he said. 'But I have to try.'

"The menehune thought for a while and went to talk to his friends. They came back to Laka with an offer. 'We can shape a canoe. We can haul it to the ocean. We will do this for you tonight.'

"Laka didn't know what to say. 'What can I do for you? I don't have much to offer.'

"'Build a shed for the canoe,' the menehune said. 'And prepare a feast for us. That is all we ask.'

"Now, that was something Laka could do. Calling out his thanks, he ran home to build the shed and prepare the feast. He stayed up all night working, setting the beams and thatching the roof with coconut fronds. In the morning, he caught fish from shore and wrapped them in tī leaves to steam them. He pounded poi and made haupia from coconuts he grated on sharp rocks. But even as he did all this work, he thought, *How is this possible? It takes months to shape a canoe; even I know that.* But he spread out the feast on a lauhala mat next to the new shed, and then, unable to stay on his feet any longer, he fell asleep.

"When Laka woke in the morning, he was surrounded by the villagers. 'Laka!' they said. 'You built such an incredible canoe!' Laka looked past them to where a perfectly shaped and cured canoe was resting in the shed, its ama firmly lashed in place. Laka struggled to his feet and stepped over the remains of the feast he had left the night before, all the food long gone. He ran his hands along the sides of the canoe, feeling how perfectly smooth and balanced it was.

"'It wasn't me,' he said at last. 'It was the menehune, and they did it all in one night.'"

"Thanks, Dad," I said softly.

He shrugged. "Sure, no worries."

Mom leaned over to give me a kiss and a hug. "That was a great idea, Emma. I haven't heard that story in years."

"Um," I said, thinking fast. "I have, uh, another great idea? Since we're over here, can we go see that heiau? You know, the one the menehune built?"

Dad frowned. "Moʻokini? That's all the way in North Kohala. It's literally the farthest north we can get and still be on the island. We need to go to Costco."

"Please? It's important."

"Why do you want to go to Moʻokini?" Mom asked gently. I looked up at her, and she looked steadily back at me. Neither of us said anything, but I knew she must be thinking about what I'd told them, about menehune. I didn't think this meant she believed me necessarily, but at least she was paying attention.

After a moment, she turned to my dad. "Let's go. It's early still, and we're not in a hurry."

"What? Leave the beach already?"

"Oh, come on, it's not like you even want to stay. Do you?"

"Well, no," Dad admitted. "But neither do I want to drive half an hour in the wrong direction and then hike in the hot sun just to go see a heiau." But he stood and began folding his chair, packing up.

I could have hugged them both, but I tried to appear calm. "Thanks, guys. I really appreciate it."

It *was* a hot hike, and to Dad's credit he didn't complain. Much. Most of Kohala is gorgeous, green, and lush with slopes of grassy hills and dramatic valleys, the sharp edges of the island carved by hundreds of thousands of years of wind and rain. But the shoreline we walked along was dusty and rocky, with no shade. There wasn't even anywhere to jump into the water to cool off—everything was rock or cliff face. When we finally got to Moʻokini, there wasn't much to indicate what we were looking at, as was true at most heiau on the island. There was a small sign offering the name of the place, and that was it. The heiau itself was tall, sometimes seven feet and sometimes as high as fourteen feet, and it was constructed entirely of black lava rock—something that wasn't easily found in Kohala, the oldest part of the island.

I didn't know anything about it except that it was old and had supposedly been built by menehune. Mom pulled up Google on her phone. "It's one of the oldest heiau in the islands, and one of the most sacred," she read. "It was dedicated to Kū, the god of war. It says that the rocks used to build it were passed hand to hand, one by one, all the way from Niuliʻi." She looked up. "That's ten miles away."

I reached out and touched the wall, the heat of the sharp black rocks pressing against my palm. "And they did it all in one night."

Mom looked at me sharply. "Yes. That's the legend, anyway."

After a while, Mom and Dad went to sit in the shadow cast by the wall of the heiau while I walked around. I looked at the rocks, the size and weight of them. The thing about lava rock is sometimes it can be disarmingly light, so porous that it seems to weigh almost nothing. But the lava flow isn't consistent, and sometimes you've got a rock that looks like any other but is so dense it weighs much more than it seems like it should. The smaller āʻā rocks crunched under my slippers, and I had to walk carefully so I didn't trip and cut myself. I looked at the construction of the temple, how it was wide at the base with heavier rocks at the bottom, so that it could taper in as it grew upward. I looked at the enormous altar stone and couldn't imagine how anyone could have lifted it.

"Okay," I said at last. "We can go to Costco now."

CHAPTER SIXTEEN

AFTER I'D HELPED UNLOAD A COUPLE OF very large bottles of vodka, a case of wine, a case of coconut milk, a giant tub of laundry soap, and several restaurant-sized bottles of olive oil (my mom lives in constant fear of an olive-oil shortage), I asked for permission to go out to the forest after dinner.

I could tell my mom really, *really* wanted to say no, but she instead offered, "I'll drive you. *After* I shower off the sand."

Duly cleaned and fed, we drove up to the construction site. Mom had brought a thermos of tea, and she leaned against the car to wait for me. It was misting heavily, and she pulled up the hood of her raincoat. "Stay where I can see you," she said.

I bit my lip. Maybe I would get another fern impersonator? But that wasn't something I could count on. "Um. I don't think that will be possible? But I'm just going in the woods there." I pointed in the direction of the lava tube.

Mom shook her head. "Nope, not happening. How about I come with you?"

By this point, I was basically twitching with impatience and frustration. Seriously, the characters in my books never had to deal with this sort of nonsense from their parents. I had *things to do*.

But I knew that saying so would only make things worse. "I don't think that's going to work." I spoke calmly as possible. "The people I need to see—"

"The menehune," Mom said flatly.

"Yes, the menehune. They don't . . . well, I don't think they'll want to be seen by someone who . . ."

"Who what?"

"Who doesn't necessarily believe in them?" I couldn't think how else to put it. Koa wasn't the most patient of people, and I didn't think he'd be willing to suffer the lengthy and inevitable questioning my mom would put him through. She wasn't an expert at cross-examination for nothing.

My mom closed her eyes and took a sip of tea before answering. "Emma. I walked several miles in the hot sun today. I am now standing in the rain when I would *much* rather be home watching reruns of *Downton Abbey*. Exactly how much do I have to prove myself to you?"

Ouch. And fair point.

"But you didn't believe me before—" I said slowly.

"But I'm trying now!" she said, exasperated.

"*Trying* to believe doesn't mean believing!" I took a breath and made an effort to sound calmer. "What do you think is going to happen if I go into the woods by myself?"

Mom looked away. "Nothing, probably," she said at last.

"Then can I go? Please?"

Her eyes slid back to look at me, and I met her gaze, blinking against the droplets of rain blowing into my eyes.

"I'm setting a timer on my phone," she said, resigned. "You'd better be back in half an hour, or I'm coming looking for you."

"Okay! Thanks, Mom!"

She flapped a hand at me and climbed back into the car to keep dry while she waited. I took off across the cleared field at a jog. By this point, I knew my way to the lava tube fairly well, and I didn't need night vision to move through the woods without stumbling. When I got there, I found a group of a dozen or so menehune milling around outside the tunnel, all talking at once. I didn't see Koa among them.

"Hi, excuse me? Is Koa around?"

They turned around, looking at me suspiciously.

I recognized Lanakila, the young menehune girl-woman who had challenged Koa. "We don't need you here anymore," she said. "We can handle this on our own."

"Not like she was doing anything anyway," another one muttered.

I bit my lip. "I know. I mean, I tried, but . . . anyway, I have an idea of how to help now. Koa told me why you can't leave, but maybe there's a way after all. Can I talk to him, please?"

Lanakila shook her head. "Koa has better things to do than waste time talking to you. Go home."

She turned her back to me, pointedly, and the voices began rising in talk again.

"But Lanakila, we were *seen*."

She shrugged. "So? It changes nothing. We do what needs to be done."

"But Koa said—"

"Enough about Koa," Lanakila snapped. "He's the one who suggested we sabotage the machines. So that's what we're doing."

The menehune who had interrupted her pushed on. "But he *also* said that we must never, ever be seen. And that man, Kainoa, he saw us!"

"He doesn't know what he saw," Lanakila said, dismissive. "Besides, Koa is the one who started letting us be seen." She turned back to me, sneering. "And now we've got her hanging around here all the time. What did I tell you?" she snapped at me. "Go away."

In the crowd of menehune, I could see some who looked hesitant. Worried. But most of them looked angry, and relieved to finally be *doing* something rather than just waiting for more human destruction. I couldn't blame them, though my gut felt hollow and cold at the idea of them being seen by someone like Kainoa.

Another menehune, larger and older-looking than Lanakila, though not by much, stepped forward. "She said to leave. So leave."

When I got back to the car, well within my half-hour allotment, my mom took one look at my face and didn't say anything. She just squeezed my hand and drove us home. I sat and watched *Downton Abbey* with her in thanks, but I couldn't follow what was going on. My mind and heart were somewhere else.

I couldn't sleep that night. Obviously, I didn't feel all that warm and fuzzy toward Lanakila and her friends, but I understood where they were coming from, and I was worried about them. I didn't think they fully understood the risks involved in what they were doing. And where was Koa?

I finally dragged myself out of bed when the sun came up, exhausted from trying to sleep for so long. I poured myself a milk-sugar-coffee and blearily inquired as to the day's planned wedding chores.

My mom gave me a little squeeze around the shoulders and slid a bowl of yogurt in front of me. "Nothing too strenuous. The hydrangeas for the favors are finally dry, so we're going to be putting them together today. Getting down to the last-minute stuff!"

Her voice was so bright and excited I could tell there was panic underneath. I took a bracing sip and tried to sound energetic and capable. "We've got this, Mom. It's going to be great."

"I know!" she said, sounding even more cheery, which I didn't think was possible. Bad sign. I wolfed down my yogurt, put the bowl in the sink, and then walked into the dining room, where all the stuff for the favors had been spread out.

There was a big pile of dried hydrangea. There were ferns and piles of human-made sea glass (well, all sea glass was human-made, I supposed—but this was purchased sea glass, not foraged). There were bags and bags of chocolate-covered macadamias. A corresponding number of little cellophane baggies. There were tiny little lauhala gift boxes. And there was raffia. So much raffia.

I took a big gulp of coffee. "Right, okay. Some assembly required."

I queued up some Beamer Brothers and got to work. Four chocolate-covered macadamias in a bag, tie with raffia. Place in bottom half of box. Carefully add a small cluster of dried hydrangea. Be careful not to squash. Add ferns and sea glass. Cover with the top of the box, tie with more raffia. Repeat *forever*.

I'd been at it for what felt like a hundred years but was probably just about an hour when there was a knock on the door. I got up to answer it, eager for a break, but my mom waved me back to work. Tyrant.

It was probably just one of my aunts or uncles dropping by. I hummed along with "Seabreeze" and tried to make a game of how I tied the raffia. It was a very boring game.

A hand dropped onto my shoulder, and I jumped. "Emma," Mom said. "There's someone to see you."

I craned my neck to look out the kitchen door.

Hilo stood there, hovering awkwardly in the doorway.

"Hey, girl," he said.

I jumped up, knocking boxes and things everywhere, and ran to the door, throwing my arms around him. He huffed a laugh and brought his arms up around my back, squeezing tight. I pulled back, grinning, and then flushed a little when I realized how close his face was to mine. He looked a lot better when he wasn't covered in dirt. I dropped my arms quickly and stepped back.

"Do you want to come in?"

Hilo kicked off his slippers and walked in, closing the door behind him. "I'm sorry it took so long for me to come by—it took me a while to remember where you lived."

"It's fine," I said, too brightly. I took a deep, steadying breath. "Do you want something to drink?"

He shook his head. "I'm good, thanks."

My mom cleared her throat, and I turned to see an amused expression on her face. "Alika, come all the way in, won't you? You'll have to excuse the mess—we're getting ready for my older daughter's wedding. It's in two days, if you can believe it. And she and her fiancée are arriving today!"

I glanced at her sharply, hearing that hysterical note coming back into her voice. "I've got time to hang out with my friend, though, *right, Mom*?"

She raised her hands in defense. "Absolutely. Take your time. I'll just . . ." She started to back out of the kitchen.

"Can I help?" Hilo offered.

"Oh, no need," I said.

"Oh, how nice of you!" Mom said simultaneously.

We glared at each other, and suddenly Hilo grinned, relaxed at last. "I'd be happy to help. I promise."

And that was how poor Hilo got roped into putting together wedding favors with me. He genuinely didn't seem to mind, though—we set up an assembly line, with me doing the chocolate things and him doing the boxes. He tied a defter and prettier raffia knot than I did, so we figured it was best to have him do the part that would show. My mom kept us supplied with a steady stream of snacks, and Hilo hijacked the speaker to play music he claimed people on the mainland listened to these days. It was certainly nothing that got any radio play around here.

"You seem a lot better," I said shyly.

He laughed. "You mean I don't seem completely out of my mind? Yeah. It took a little while, but I got clearer every day. My poor parents—they took me to doctors and stuff, and all anyone could say was 'trauma.' Which wasn't at all helped by me rambling about trees and menehune."

I looked around to check for my mom, but she was outside. "Yeah, I hear you. Nobody would believe me, either. I mean, my parents know *something* is going on, but they're not sure what to think."

Hilo nodded. "That's pretty much how my parents feel at this point, too. That's the other reason I was so long in coming," he said, sounding awkward. "It took a while to persuade them to let me. My dad said he talked to you, and you seemed nice, but my mom kind of wanted to keep me away from anything that was related to the time I was lost, like that would cause a relapse or something."

"I get that," I said softly.

Hilo reached out to fiddle with a cellophane bag, and it crunched loudly in his fingers. "It wasn't right, though. You helped me. And . . . and we still have things to do."

I sighed and leaned back in my chair. "Yeah, well, I haven't had a lot of luck with that, either." I told him about the heiau Koa had shown me, and about Lanakila and her friends sabotaging the equipment at the site.

Hilo frowned. "That doesn't sound very safe. When I was out doing that stuff with Koa, he was always so careful. *We cannot be seen*—he said that again and again."

"I know." Eyeing the still pitifully small pile of completed favors, I went back to tying cellophane. "And the thing is, I have this idea that might help. But I couldn't get them to listen to me."

I handed him a finished bag of chocolate-covered mac nuts, and his fingers brushed against my wrist as he took them. "Tell me your idea," he said.

CHAPTER SEVENTEEN

"I'LL WORK," HILO INSISTED. "I MEAN, YOU'RE right, we're definitely going to need help, and that will require people who are willing to listen and believe us...."

"Which seems unlikely," I said.

"Which seems unlikely," Hilo admitted. "But it's still the best idea we've got. Anyway, nothing else has worked. We should go tell Koa."

"I *tried*," I said, exasperated. "That's why I went there last night. But he wasn't even there!"

"He was probably off doing something," Hilo said reasonably. "We can go again. We've got"—he eyed the remaining pile of empty lauhala boxes—"a bunch more to do, but we'll finish by lunch probably? We can go after. My dad needs me to pick him up after his shift anyway."

I think my mom was so relieved to have had Hilo's help that she didn't put up a single argument when I asked if we could leave. I climbed into Hilo's beige Nissan Xterra and watched his hands as he started it up, confident and at ease. He put his arm around my seat as he backed down my driveway, and I pressed my hands under my thighs to keep them still. We went first to Uncle Danny's store to grab lunch. There weren't any musubi left, sadly, but my uncle microwaved us some frozen burritos and let me take a bag of arare rice crackers. If you dump them into the burrito, they give it a bit more texture and flavor.

We ate sitting in the back of the car, the trunk open and our legs dangling over the side. We didn't talk much, but that was okay—it was a comfortable sort of silence, the kind that happens when you don't need to fill it with anything that doesn't matter.

When we finished, Hilo took my rubbish and tossed it into the bin, then took my hand and pulled me around to the driver's side door. "Climb in," he said.

I gaped at him. "I don't know if you remember this, but the first time we met I almost hit you with my car. I don't think you want me driving."

"Oh, I remember," Hilo said, grinning. "You were more terrified than I was." He cocks his head at the door. "Go on. We have about two hours to kill before we can go pick up my dad. Plenty of time for practice."

With a helpless sigh, I climbed up and into the SUV and fastened my seat belt. Hilo handed me the keys, and I started it up. I was seated a lot higher than when I drove the RAV4, and the size of the car made me nervous—any car was capable of killing someone, but this one felt like it could do even more damage.

"You're going to be fine," Hilo said. I wished I had his confidence.

I backed carefully out of the stall, and now it was my arm flung around Hilo's seat. I pulled out of the parking lot and onto Old Volcano Road. "Where to?" I asked.

"What do you struggle with most?"

I took a deep breath. Where to begin? "Parallel parking," I said, which wasn't a lie, but wasn't the truth, either.

"Okay," Hilo said, nodding. "We can work on that. What else?"

"Passing. Changing lanes. Reversing." I began to babble, the list going on and on, until it included pretty much every single aspect of driving a car. And Hilo just listened, giving me quiet instructions like "Turn here" whenever necessary. "I'm afraid of what a car can do," I said, telling the truth at last. "I . . . I get distracted sometimes. I daydream. And I'm worried if I get distracted at the wrong time, then—" My voice broke, but Hilo finished the sentence for me.

"Then you'll get into an accident," he said quietly. "And someone might get hurt."

I nodded, my throat too full to speak. I paused at a stop sign, looked both ways—there was no one coming—and kept going.

"I get that," Hilo said. "But Emma, people drive every day, millions and millions of people. And you're absolutely right, car accidents happen every day, too—but not so many that it's not worth doing. You're a really thoughtful person. You care so much—it's why I trusted you even when I couldn't trust myself. You should trust yourself, too."

I drove for a while longer, round and round in circles, weaving my way around the village. Then, with a deep breath and a glance at Hilo for permission, I pulled out onto the highway. The engine roared beneath my feet, the car accelerating as I brought it up to speed. I felt the centrifugal force as I took the sharp right turn that meant we were approaching the national park, then continued on down the highway past the gated entrance, the trees whipping by.

I'd driven on the highway before during driver's ed, the instructor urging me to press on the gas. "Gas to go," she'd said, again and again. And my dad, trying to teach me, would flex his hands against his legs, as if restraining himself from reaching for the parking brake. Hilo didn't do anything of the sort—he just relaxed in his seat, arms crossed over his chest. "Turn here," he said eventually.

I turned into the golf-course subdivision, a different side of Volcano that felt more suburban than a community so isolated had any right to. Mauna Loa stretched over the horizon, effortlessly elegant against the blue sky. I drove into one of the many cul-de-sacs and practiced pulling up alongside the curb. Hilo put his slippers down to serve as markers and talked me through parallel parking as he stood barefoot in the street. We practiced over and over, and Hilo never showed signs of frustration or even impatience with me. And slowly, my confidence grew, and I began to be able to laugh and talk and drive without clutching the steering wheel so tightly the whites of my knuckles showed.

As I got more comfortable behind the wheel, I grew more and more aware of how close it was in the car, just the two of us. How Hilo put an arm around the back of my seat to check to make sure no one was coming up behind us, and how he left it there, and I could feel his fingers brushing my hair. Whenever I glanced over at him, he looked back at me, and it became just a little hard to breathe.

As the afternoon wore down to an end, I drove us back to the village, up Wright Road to where I could pull off the road, the large wheels of the Xterra moving smoothly over the gravel parking lot that had been laid down.

As we got out of the car, Hilo spotted his dad and gave him a wave—Mr. Kaneshiro wiped his forehead with his sleeve and waved back. I saw Kainoa standing there, doing nothing as usual, just watching us. I ignored him and pulled Hilo along the road. I didn't want Kainoa to see where we were going. I didn't know what he would do if he found out about the lava tube the menehune were living in. I didn't want to know.

We walked away from where they were working, off into a corner of the site where some equipment stood unused, sidling our way toward the entrance to the lava tube. Over the course of the afternoon, the sun had given way to cloud cover, and here in the village it was a little wet out, with that drizzly rain that still lets enough sunlight through so you have to squint. It felt like you needed sunglasses *and* a raincoat, and since I hadn't bothered with either I was just wet and squinty. It was hard to make it out at first, but there was the backhoe, sitting at the corner of the clearing. As I looked closer, I noticed a rock about three feet tall, tied with a rope to the backhoe. What was it?

We moved even closer, and I started shaking as my brain began to fully process what we were looking at. The realization seemed to hit Hilo at the same time. He grabbed my arm, and I turned my face into his shoulder, trying to push back my scream. I couldn't look anymore.

It was Lanakila. It was hard to tell at first because it wasn't like she had turned into some exquisitely carved statue like in the White Witch's courtyard in Narnia. No, she had turned to lava rock, lumpy and porous and indistinct. But there was the drooping cuff of her too-big sweatshirt. Her eyes, once deep-set and fierce, were now nothing but black, pitted holes.

I cried as Hilo dragged me deeper into the woods, pulling me out of sight of Kainoa and his dad and everyone else. "Come on," he said, over and over. We headed for the lava tube, as if everything would be all right there and we could pretend this hadn't happened.

When we made it to the entrance, Hilo left me sitting on a log and ran in to get Koa, or anyone, whomever he could find. I thought that was what he was doing, anyway. I just sat there, plucking at the moss covering the fallen hāpuʻu, feeling the wet soaking into my jeans. I heard the birds singing overhead, twittering in call and response, heard their wings fluttering as they moved from branch to branch. A red 'apapane fluttered down to eye level, cocking its head at me, as if to ask, *What did you do?*

I looked away.

"Koa won't come out," Hilo said as he returned to me, his voice rough. "He says they can't. Daylight, he says."

A drip of rainwater ran into my eye, and I blinked. Of course. I should have realized.

"Come on," Hilo said again. He pulled me up off my log and led me into the lava tube. It didn't take long for the light to fade and for us to be in complete darkness. I sensed movement without seeing it, and then my eyes switched to menehune sight as Koa stepped forward.

"Lanakila," I blurted.

"I know," he said quietly. "She went out with some others last night, without my knowledge. They were seen." He began to walk into the tunnel, and, not knowing what else to do, we followed him.

The menehune were subdued. Some of them were quietly weeping. I saw a few of the menehune I'd talked with the night before sitting alone in a corner, huddled around a giant old wooden spool, a reel used to hold wire or cables, though they were using it as a table. Koa kept walking, reaching out to clasp hands as he moved through his people, but not stopping and not saying anything.

My eyes began to burn, and I realized that I was seeing light up ahead. Koa stopped at the edge of the big cathedral room, and I followed his gaze. In the tunnel just ahead, the ceiling had collapsed, leaving another skylight.

"But . . . that's where you sleep," I said stupidly.

"Not anymore," Koa said, grim. "The room behind us is all we have left now. There are too many openings. Soon enough, the light will come in there, too, and we will all be as Lanakila."

"That won't happen," Hilo said. "I promise you. Emma has a plan. If we can just—"

He stopped, and in the silence I heard it. Someone was shouting, and the sound was drifting down through the skylight.

"That's my dad," Hilo said, turning to run back through the lava tube.

I followed him, hurrying to keep up as he burst out into the forest. I blinked as my eyes adjusted, trying not to trip as we ran between the trees, ducking under branches.

"What is wrong with you? Do you have no soul? 'Uhane 'ole?" I watched as quiet, calm Mr. Kaneshiro grabbed Kainoa by the jacket, shoving him up against the backhoe. "What did you do?" Alika's dad shouted.

Kainoa shoved him off. "What I had to," he said coldly, straightening his jacket. "Management was all over me, wanting to know what was causing the delays. They were going to pull our funding; do you get that? What would that mean for you, for all of you? I am responsible for making sure *you* get paid."

"But that was a menehune," Mr. Kaneshiro said brokenly.

I don't know how Mr. Kaneshiro knew—Lanakila didn't even look like herself anymore. She was just a stone, unless you gazed at her with eyes that chose to see the magic. Hilo ran up to his dad, panting, moving himself between the two men. *Oh, God*, I thought, trailing after him. Kainoa. He must have stayed late at the site, watching for sabotage. And Lanakila, reckless in her desperation, must have allowed herself to be seen—and Kainoa had tied her up with the rope and left her there. So that when the sun came up . . .

I felt a surge of bile and turned as my frozen burrito came up. I felt hands on my shoulders as Hilo held me, steadying me. I watched as Mr. Kaneshiro slowly turned away from Kainoa.

"You walk off this job, and you won't walk back on," Kainoa warned.

Mr. Kaneshiro kept walking, and Hilo and I followed him. He climbed into the truck and held his hand out for the keys. Hilo gave them to him without a word. As we drove away, I heard the rumble of machinery starting up again.

I wanted—needed—to tell everyone everything, about Lanakila and what was happening to the menehune, but as soon as Hilo's dad dropped me off at home, I knew that wasn't going to be possible right now.

The moment I opened the door, my sister let out a scream and threw her arms around me. I'd forgotten—

how could I have forgotten?—that my dad was picking Puʻulena and Naomi up from the airport today. And they were so excited. I mean, Puʻulena isn't exactly a bubbly person, and Naomi can be kind of reserved until you get to know her, but they were practically effervescent. Talking over each other, asking questions, making plans, laughing—it was like they'd had three cups of coffee apiece, jet lag be damned. I was quiet—I couldn't help it—but nobody noticed in the general clamor.

My parents put out wine and cheese and Triscuits, and my dad cooked ahi with capers—my sister's favorite—and we sat around the kitchen table. There were only five of us, but they were all talking so loudly I couldn't hear *Born to Run* playing underneath—also my sister's favorite. After dinner, Puʻulena pulled Naomi onto her lap to force her to stay when my dad brought out the cards. Naomi wasn't so much for games, but the love language of my family was trash talk, particularly over card games. With Naomi on Puʻulena's "team," as it were, I couldn't sit out or we wouldn't have enough people.

"I wouldn't do that if I were you, Victoria. Emma's got the ace."

"You don't know that. How do you know that?" my mom demanded.

"Because I pay attention," my dad said, laughing.

As it happened, I did have the ace, and when I played it, my dad did his signature celebratory dance complete with gorilla arms and tree-monkey noises.

"Oh yeah?" Puʻulena said slyly. And she threw down a trump card.

"Whoooaaaaa!" my dad yelled, and my mom cackled. I don't think she cared as much about winning the game as she did about beating my dad.

"Why would a four beat an ace?" Naomi asked, and my sister threw her head back in her chair, exasperated.

"We've been together for how many years? We are *getting married in two days*. How do you not get this?"

Naomi shrugged and kissed my sister on the temple. "It's more fun to bother you than to pay attention."

I tried to join in; I really did. Ordinarily, I'd have been needling Puʻulena and poking fun at my mom and joining in with the gorilla dance. And I wanted to do all of that. I knew how much Puʻulena missed this when she was away, and the reality was that now that she was getting married, she would never move home again, which made nights like this even *more* important. But it was all I could do to fake a smile and play the game without bursting into tears.

After my dad and I lost the second round in a row—my fault entirely—I excused myself and went to my room. I didn't do anything, just stood there listening to the rain hitting the roof, the light cloud cover of the late afternoon having grown heavy and saturated as the sun went down. Rain was not an unusual thing in Hawaiʻi, certainly. But this rain was unusual even for us. It was the kind of rain that hurt when it hit the back of your neck, slapping you with so much water you were instantly wet. It was ua hōʻeʻele, the kind of rain that struck the roof so loudly it roared and you had to speak up to be heard over it. It was an angry rain, and I couldn't help but think it was the skies weeping for Lanakila.

I had meant to be there for only a minute, just long enough to get myself together. But when Naomi knocked on the door and poked her head in, I didn't have time to pause the flood of emotions, and my face crumpled as the tears I'd been holding back started to fall.

Naomi didn't say anything. She just threw her arms around me and let me cry until I was able to speak.

"I'm sorry," I said finally, sniffling.

"It's completely okay," she murmured. "I knew something was up with you. What is it? Is it the wedding? You know we'll come to visit all the time, right?"

I gave her a squeeze. "I know, and I promise it's not that. I mean, I'll miss her, but I'm so happy for you both."

She pulled back a little to look at my face. "Then what is it, Em? Something isn't right. Can you come tell us about it?"

I heard the laughter coming from the kitchen and shrugged helplessly. Naomi glanced over her shoulder and shook her head. "They would want to know; you know they would. You're not ruining anything, okay? I promise."

Naomi escorted me into the kitchen, and as soon as Puʻulena and my mom saw my red eyes, they switched immediately from laughing to concern. It took my dad a few more moments to notice, but I think my mom kicked him under the table. Puʻulena nodded encouragingly.

I took a deep breath. "I need to talk to you guys about what's been happening the past few weeks. And I need you to listen all the way to the end. And then I need your help."

CHAPTER EIGHTEEN

I TOOK THEM UP TO SEE THE ROCK THAT WAS now Lanakila. It was dark out, so it was kind of hard to see, but at least the rain had settled to a gentler fall. My mom reached out a hand and stroked the top of Lanakila's head. My dad's hands bunched into fists as he shoved them into the pockets of his coat. Puʻulena put her arm around me.

"Do you believe me now?" I asked quietly.

My mom tilted her head up at the sky, her eyes closed against the droplets.

"It's a rock, Emma," my dad said gently. Puʻulena started to argue, but he held up a hand. "But maybe it wasn't always. And maybe belief isn't about being certain. Maybe it's about choosing to have faith, and, Emma, I will always have faith in you." He pulled me in for a hug, and my mom came around behind me, sandwiching me in their arms like they used to do when I was little. Puʻulena and Naomi joined in, and I felt them all standing around me, holding me up.

My mom sniffled a little when we finally pulled back, and I could have sworn I saw my dad wipe his eyes. "What can we do to help?" Mom asked.

At first, it wasn't that different from calling everyone to come protest at the construction site. Basically, Mom called her family, and then she called Auntie Mele, who pretty much took it from there. I called Ana, and she put me on speaker to talk to her parents directly, since it was a pretty big ask. Puʻulena called some of her friends from high school, and I called Hilo to see if he had talked to anyone. He had, and his father had, and some—not all—of the other workers on the site were going to come help.

It was late by the time everyone got there, which worried me. Every hour meant one less hour before daylight. But Ana and her parents came, having driven all that way. I introduced Hilo to Ana and Puʻulena, and while I'm pretty sure I blushed, it was absolutely for no reason, and anyway in that moment I was just a little bit grateful for the darkness. By this time, the rain had stopped entirely, and the moon occasionally poked through the clouds.

Auntie Mele put herself in charge of organizing, which was good because not everyone who had shown up was going to be able to help. The adults and older kids, sure, but some of the people who came, like my cousins, had babies, and someone had to keep an eye on them while everyone else worked. Uncle Mike came with his big truck, and I didn't know if we would be allowed to use it, but if so, it sure would be a help, and I appreciated the risk he was taking. The risk everyone involved with the site was taking. Uncle Danny brought his entire stock of flashlights and rope, and Auntie Paula had filled the big yellow-and-red water cooler they used for church picnics and soccer games so we would all stay hydrated.

All told, it was probably around fifty people. I hoped it would be enough.

Hilo nudged me. "You have to make a speech."

I went pale in the cloudy moonlight. "What? Absolutely not."

"Emma, they're mostly your people. And it's your plan. I'll come with you to talk to Koa, but this part should be you."

He boosted me up to stand in the bed of Uncle Mike's truck and cupped his hands. "Hūi! Everybody, thanks so much for coming. Emma's going to explain what we're all doing here."

Right. I was going to explain.

They shined their flashlights at me, creating a multi-faceted spotlight and blinding me in the process. "Um. Hi. Yeah, thanks for coming. And, uh, as to why you're here . . ." I squinted and looked down to see Hilo in the shadows by the bumper of the truck. "We're here because we've messed up. All of us. Some of you know Hilo, I mean, Alika. He messed up and he paid the price for it. He made his amends, and he's fine now. But we've all done things we regret, chipping away at our own autonomy. We take jobs we don't want; we accept changes on the islands we don't want and didn't ask for. But some of what we're doing isn't just hurting us; it's also hurting our land and the . . ." I swallowed hard. "The people that live here, protecting us and our home. It's not our fault. We didn't ask to be colonized, for our language and our storytelling and our traditions to be erased. But it happened, and maybe there isn't much of anything we can do about it now. But sometimes maybe we can. Maybe sometimes we can make amends for the mistakes we have made, for the hard choices we were forced into. And maybe we can work to protect the people who have been protecting us and help them for a change."

"What people, Emma?" Uncle Danny asked. "What are you talking about?"

"Over here," my sister called. She and Naomi shined their flashlights on Lanakila. "She's talking about menehune."

There was a pause, and then an awkward laugh that was followed by another, and another.

"It's true," Hilo's dad said. "I believe it."

"Um, that's a rock," Ikaika said. I glared at him.

Everyone started talking at once then, arguing and laughing nervously and shivering in the cold and wondering what the hell they'd been thinking when they'd picked up the phone that night. They milled around me as I stood awkwardly in the truck bed. Hilo climbed up to stand beside me, our shoulders touching. "I don't know how to make them believe," he said quietly. "Will they even be able to see the menehune if they don't?"

"Maybe they don't need to believe enough to see the menehune," I said slowly. "They just need to believe enough to help."

"Okay," Hilo said, doubtful. "But how do we do that?"

"Just . . . please follow us," I called across the field. "I know it sounds crazy, and I know it's late and dark and you'd much rather be home, but you've come all this way. Please come just a little farther."

Some people stayed behind, but most of them did come, albeit slowly, following Hilo and me into the forest. We picked a trail that led away from the opening to the lava tube where the menehune lived . . . sort of. It was impossible to get where we were going without walking close by. But I swore the trees moved for us, just a little, clearing a path that was, if not easy to follow in the darkness, at least possible. I wondered what the trail of flashlights through the forest looked like from the sky.

We made it to the heiau Koa had shown me, and everyone filed in, standing in an unconsciously reverent half circle around it.

"Did you know this was here?" I heard my mom ask Uncle Mike.

"No," he said, sounding taken aback. "I've never seen it before, and I've been all through these woods."

Thankfully, this heiau wasn't a large luakini like Mo'okini. There was a platform, about three feet high, with walls of about six feet on every side and a doorway entrance. There were smaller, unwalled platforms on either side.

It might have been small, but it was still a lot of rock.

I cleared my throat. "Okay, so . . . what we need to do is move this heiau. It doesn't really matter if you believe me about the menehune—this heiau can't stay here. With all the activity and construction going on, you can see how it's crumbling. And, well, it's needed elsewhere. I think . . ." I looked around at my mom and dad, at Ana, at my sister. At Hilo. At my aunts and uncles and friends and people I'd known my whole life. At strangers I'd never met, who didn't know me but were listening anyway. "I think it needs to go to Leilani Estates. I think we need to rebuild, to help the forest grow there. They need rain, and life, and our kokua. So yeah. That's what I asked you all here to do."

There was silence. It went on and on, and all I could hear was the plop of leaves falling to the ground, the shifting of someone's feet crackling the small dead branches beneath. I felt my shoulders drop, and Hilo, standing beside me, squeezed my hand. "We'll think of something else," he whispered. "It'll be okay."

But then Ana stepped forward and picked up a rock. It looked heavy, and it came from the corner of one of the anterior platforms. She passed it to her father, who looked blankly at it for a moment, but then he passed it to her mother. "Like that?" Ana said. "Like the stories say the menehune did?"

My throat closed and my eyes blurred with tears.

"Yes," Hilo said roughly. "Like that."

"Okay, but which way is Leilani Estates?" someone asked.

Uncle Mike pointed east. "It's that way. Pretty much a straight shot. But can't we just put them in my truck? And some other trucks? We don't need to go hand to hand all that way—it's got to be fifteen miles, and it's all forest reserve. It would take days."

"We don't have days," I said. "We have to do it all tonight."

More silence. "Emma, honey, I don't think that's possible," my mom said gently.

"We definitely need the trucks," my dad agreed. "And wheelbarrows. Or maybe ATVs? Who's got an ATV?"

They all started talking again, figuring out who had trucks (most of them—it was the Big Island, after all). Others started passing the rocks hand over hand, bringing them to the road, until my mom started panic-yelling.

"Stop, stop, stop! We can't just take whatever—how are we going to rebuild it?"

Oh, God. That hadn't even occurred to me. I was so concerned with just getting enough hands to get it moved, and that had definitely seemed difficult enough. But with Moʻokini, all the menehune had to do was move rocks from a valley to the shoreline, and then build from there, which obviously would take some skill—but it wasn't *re-creating* something that already existed. I didn't know what would happen if we didn't rebuild it exactly right, but I had to assume that would be bad.

All eyes turned to me, figuring that I'd thought of this, that I had a plan.

"Um," I said. "I'll be back in a minute."

I ran off into the woods, Hilo on my heels. I'd expected Koa to turn up as soon as we showed up at the heiau, but if he was being shy, we'd just have to persuade him to come out, and sooner rather than later. But as we neared the entrance to the lava tube, there was silence.

It was always quiet, but this felt different. We should have been able to hear the people talking behind us, the rustling of leaves in the breeze, even the murmuring of the menehune within. But it was like we'd entered some sort of bubble, and all sound was deadened. Disoriented, I looked to Hilo for confirmation, and his eyes were wide. He felt it, too.

I jumped at the sound of Koa's voice in the quiet. "What are you doing here?" he asked flatly.

"Koa!" I ran to him as he stood at the edge of the tube. "Why didn't you come out? Everyone's here, we're going to make it work, we—"

"Emma," he snapped. "Shut your mouth. How dare you bring all those people here?"

I stopped in my tracks. "I . . . what?"

"I trusted you, both of you. And this is what you do? You bring strangers to our heiau, our most sacred place? They're not even all Hawaiian!"

"But—"

"We want to help," Hilo said. "We all do, all those people. We're going to move the heiau; don't you see? We're going to bring it to Leilani Estates—there will be new lava tubes there where you can all live safely, and a new forest for you to tend. There are some houses left, but not many; it's mostly just forest reserve and lava. It won't get developed, not for a long time, anyway. No one will come bother you. You'll be safe."

"Safe," Koa said harshly. "We stay safe by staying hidden. I forgot that rule when I showed myself to you both, and look where it got me. One of our children has just been murdered. I'm not letting any of my people get hurt again."

I couldn't draw breath. My chest felt like it was folding in on itself.

"That's not what will happen! I promise, we just want to help!" Hilo sounded desperate. "It's a good plan, and you know you can't stay here!"

Koa's shoulders sagged. "I know. But my people are in mourning, and they are frightened. I can't leave them, and I can't ask them to risk any more than they already have." He sighed, defeated. I had never heard Koa sound like that, not even earlier tonight when his home was caving in around him and his people were grieving and frightened. It was as if this last blow—strangers in his forest, a perceived betrayal—was simply too much for him. "Do what you will," he said, and turned back into the lava tube.

"But . . . but wait!" I called. "We can't do this without you! You're menehune, you . . . you know stuff, like how to build heiau and how to move things—we don't know how. We're trying to do it, but this is menehune magic, and . . . and we're just people."

Koa kept walking.

CHAPTER NINETEEN

HILO AND I MADE OUR WAY BACK TO THE heiau in silence. But the moment we crossed out of Koa's barrier, the movement, voices, and noises of everyone we'd left there came back to full volume, almost deafening in contrast. There was so much happening. People were stringing up the ropes Uncle Danny had brought, to serve as guidelines on the path back to the trucks. Uncle Mike was hanging lights illuminating the heiau. People were measuring and measuring again and placing markers on keystone rocks. And my mom, that obsessive, shower-retiling, garage-cleaning queen of logistics, was right at the center of it all, giving instructions, taking pictures on her phone, and drawing a map of what went where.

Tears sprang to my eyes. I reached out to grab Hilo's hand, and he squeezed it tightly. And then we got to work.

It wasn't easy, and it definitely would have been better if we'd had the menehune helping us. But at the same time, it felt easier than it should have. The trees were making way for us, like they had when I moved through the woods with Koa. Obstacles that should have been there were gone, as if the fallen logs and sudden drops and rises in the landscape had rolled aside and smoothed out. Once my mom was satisfied with the architectural plans she'd created, we began to move the rocks, carefully and in order, passing them hand to hand down the trail to the waiting trucks.

I stood between Naomi and Ana's mom, passing rock after rock, light ones, heavy ones, larger ones and smaller ones, over and over and over again until my hands began to scrape and bleed. Someone eventually brought water and work gloves, organized by Auntie Mele, of course. We were farther down the trail, away from the lit heiau, and had very little light to see by, but it didn't seem to matter. The clouds had cleared, and the moonlight that filtered through the trees was so much brighter than it should have been, bright like one of those old movies my mom liked to watch, where they filmed during the day but put a filter on to make it seem like it was night.

Eventually the first truck was loaded, and a group of people peeled off to find an appropriate place in Leilani Estates to rebuild. My dad hollered at me to come, and I almost refused. I mean, I had *absolutely no idea* how to determine the proper site for a heiau. That was supposed to be Koa's job, and if it wasn't Koa, it should be my dad, or Mr. Kaneshiro, or Auntie Mele, or literally anyone else. But Naomi gently pushed me forward, passing her rock straight to Ana's mom, and yes, this had been my idea, hadn't it?

I made it out to Uncle Mike's truck to find it packed with rocks arranged carefully in rows, each row labeled according to my mom's system. They were starting on a second truck already. A dozen of us carpooled in a couple of packed cars—I wasn't even sure whose. Mom and Dad and Ana and Puʻulena were with me, and Kazuo, the nice man who worked at the post office, was driving. Hilo and his parents and some other people I didn't know drove off with one of the construction guys.

It took about half an hour to drive to Leilani Estates, and while there wasn't any traffic at this time of night, neither was the forest able to magically speed up our progress. Uncle Mike led the way, driving his truck through newly constructed "roads" created by dozers that essentially just crunched the lava down to gravel. Occasionally it opened up to show the paved road beneath, gaps in the hardened lava, and we would have a few hundred yards of smooth riding before the road was covered up again.

We had long since driven into an area where we definitely weren't supposed to be, but Uncle Mike was taking us through the meandering paths the county had created to take down the half-burned houses—the paths he'd used to pull out the abandoned and burned cars. Eventually, though, we ran out of road.

We climbed out of the car and joined Uncle Mike at the edge of the lava field. He'd taken us to the place where the flow met the edge of Puna Forest Reserve. We stood in the kind of loose semicircle people tend to form when they stand together. This forest was different from the one in Volcano—there were still ʻōhiʻa trees, but they were of a spindlier variety, covered with a kind of moss that seemed more reminiscent of swamps. It probably wasn't any more humid than in Volcano—I'm not sure there *is* a place more humid than Volcano—but it was warmer, and so the air felt sticky, rather than damp.

But although it was different, it still felt . . . right. It wasn't *my* forest, but it was the cousin of my forest. I could feel the same magic living and breathing here, and I could imagine I felt the eyes of the creatures and spirits that belonged to this place watching us. It didn't feel like a welcome, exactly, but there wasn't suspicion, either. It felt like neutral expectation.

It also felt overwhelming. How were we to determine the right site for the heiau? I didn't know anything about why the ancient Hawaiians had built their heiau in the places they did. What made a site sacred?

"Hoo." Puʻulena let out a breath. "Well. Where should we put it? What are the criteria here?"

There was a pause. Hilo shifted his feet, the rocks crunching beneath his sneakers. My dad scratched at the back of his head. I felt my eyes beginning to burn, tears forming behind them. It was too much responsibility, too much knowledge I didn't have, too many people I'd disappoint. Too much.

Ana cleared her throat. "Well, it needs to be somewhere visible, right? In a clearing? But protected, still, surrounded by forest. And not *too* far from the flow, since the idea is to use its energy, its magic, to push the forest out and regrow the land, right? So it has to be kind of close to where we are now, not way into the forest."

"Well, that's a relief," my uncle muttered.

"Come on," Ana said. "Let's take a quick walk."

The moon still shone overhead, but not so brightly we didn't need flashlights, especially when we were climbing over lava rock. I'd heard that the flow was up to nine hundred feet thick in some places and would take twenty years to cool completely. But on the surface, it just felt like rock. I followed Ana's dancing flashlight as she headed off into the forest, the footsteps of everyone else crunching behind me. The ferns grew lower to the ground here, and they scratched at my legs as I walked through them, trying not to crush them. The ground slanted upward, at a gentle but noticeable slope. And as we walked, it seemed that the ferns thinned, creating a kind of path guiding Ana forward. Maybe we were welcome here, after all.

The slope increased, and my legs began to ache, my breath coming fast. We hadn't gone far at all, but it still felt like a very long way to carry all those rocks. And with every step, I could feel the minutes ticking by. How much night did we have left? We'd barely begun.

At last we reached a clearing, a bit smaller than the one the heiau stood in back in Volcano. My breath caught as I recognized the shadowy shape lit by moonlight in the center of the clearing. "Koa?" I whispered.

He gestured, and two more menehune stepped out from the shadows.

"Emma?" Ana asked. "What is it?"

I gestured at the menehune, but she just looked blank, and so did everyone except Hilo. "I don't think they can see them," he said.

"They won't be able to hear us, either," Koa explained. "We cannot take the risk. But . . ." He paused. "Your idea is a good one. This place," he said, gesturing to the clearing, "it can be a home for us." I spun, shining my flashlight, and realized that I could see the vast lava field through the trees. We had crested the hill, and ahead of us the ground sloped down into a crater. It was an old one, from a flow years and years ago, now reforested and full of life.

"Emma," Ana whispered. "Look."

I followed her outstretched arm, squinting in the darkness. There was movement, a tall spindly figure, like a tree seen out of the corner of your eye. And lower to the ground, something like the elongated dog that used to play with me. A pueo hooted at us, its call eerie but not frightening.

Behind me, I felt Puʻulena still. Hilo, his parents, my uncle, my parents, everyone that had driven all this way stood, breathless, motionless. The only sounds were the quiet footsteps of the creatures.

"I think this will do," my dad said at last.

"Yes," Koa answered him, though my father could not hear. "It will do."

Of course, finding the site was the easy part. With Koa's guidance, we began the hard work of unloading the truck. And when I say "unloading the truck," I mean clearing the site; measuring; marking where the corners of the heiau would go; stringing a rope between the truck and the site so no one would get lost in the dark; getting really, really clear on which rocks should come out first; and *then* taking rocks and passing them hand to hand. We hadn't even unloaded a quarter of it before the second truck arrived.

Having more people meant more hands, so we unpacked fairly quickly, and Uncle Mike drove his truck back for another load. Koa was meticulous, and so were Hōkū and Kuawa, the menehune he'd brought with him. Hilo and I ran back and forth, delivering their instructions, which, miraculously, everyone accepted even though we probably just looked like we were listening to air and making stuff up. When I wasn't speaking on behalf of the menehune, I was on rock-passing duty. It was monotonous and unending, rock after incredibly similar rock, over and over again. But it was also somewhat comforting, even joyous. I couldn't really explain it, the simple comfort in the knowledge of all those hands, working just like mine, over and over and over again, together in the dark. People I couldn't even see. People I didn't even know. Sometimes someone passed me, bringing supplies or hot tea, and it wasn't anyone I recognized. It wasn't someone I was related to or grew up with; it wasn't even someone I recognized from the construction site. A complete stranger, here because they were guided to be here, to help. More and more trucks came, headlights shining through the trees. Eventually there were so many hands to help that I didn't even need to take two steps to pass my rock to the next person—I just reached out, and they were there.

Even so, it must have been hours, so very many hours. I could feel exhaustion coming on, but it felt like it was leashed, like all the strain and worry and physical labor were being held back from me, so I couldn't really experience them, or not enough to slow me down. I guess we were all feeling like that, because no one seemed to be getting tired. I had absolutely no idea what time it was, but it had to have been long past midnight.

Eventually, though, I passed my last rock.

"That's it," someone said. "That's all of them."

And so we abandoned our places and followed the rope and the string of bright orange extension cords to the new site of the heiau. The trees had been strung up with lights powered by the trucks, which were left running, one at a time, in shifts, so they didn't run out of gas. It was like an industrial version of the twinkle lights for my sister's wedding.

I looked around, dismayed. I thought they'd be so much further along. Instead, the vast majority of the rocks we'd passed had found their way into piles (organized piles, mind you—Hōkū had a very specific system), and only a relative few of them had been laid in place.

The problem, Koa explained, was that it was not that easy to build a heiau. You couldn't just pile the rocks anykine; they had to be nestled carefully together, angles and shapes fitted like puzzle pieces, otherwise the whole thing would topple over. With Kuawa's oversight and Hilo's translation, a team had completed the first platform, but that was the easy part. The walls were much more complex and prone to collapse.

Koa pulled Hilo and me aside and showed us how to angle a rock so that it would not only stay in place but would also provide a useful base for the next layer. It was hard to do, particularly since every rock was a different shape, but once we got the hang of it, Hilo and I showed everyone else how to do it, and slowly the first wall began to rise.

I sidled over to Hilo, who was taking a quick break, sipping hot chocolate from a thermos. "How do you think it's going?"

He shrugged. "I don't know. I don't know how much time we have."

"All these years, I just thought you were talking to your imaginary friends," Ikaika said as he stooped beside us to pick up another rock.

"Some of the time I was," I said dryly.

Ikaika kicked me as he went past. "Not going to help?"

I sighed and took a quick drink from Hilo's thermos. "Yup, coming."

Hōkū and I were in charge of the eastern corner. Corners were tough, for obvious reasons—they had to be structurally sound and at the same time form, you know, a corner. But he explained that it was all about finding the right sizes and shapes and working slowly and carefully. Sometimes he picked out the correct rock for a place, and I brought it over, but after a while I learned to see as he did and could find the necessary rocks on my own.

And so we made progress, and slowly the heiau began to grow. But there was simply too much to do. Even though we were moving as quickly as we could, the placement of the rocks had to be precise, and Koa wouldn't let us take shortcuts—because what was the point of all of this if the heiau fell down in an earthquake the next time Pele got a little restless?

I could feel the edges of dawn like an itch at the back of my neck. That reined-in exhaustion was getting tighter and closer, and my muscles ached, and my eyes were dry and blurry.

I didn't see how we could make it. There simply weren't enough hours in the night to complete the task we'd set for ourselves. I squatted by my corner, rubbing my eyes. I was too tired to cry. A strong arm pulled me backward, and I ended up sitting on the ground, leaning against my dad, half in his lap.

"Look at what you did, Emma," he whispered. "Look at all these people."

I swallowed past the lump in my throat. "But it's not going to be enough," I said, my voice cracking. "There's so much more to do."

"Do you see anybody giving up?" I watched with him as men and women and kids who were old enough to help worked steadily, taking breaks when they needed to, talking easily and taking instruction from one another as they all learned together what methods worked best.

"No," I said at last. "But there isn't time. We have to get it done by morning. That's how all the stories go. And how can we? It's got to be almost sunrise."

I felt my dad shift. "Let me show you something." He pulled his arm out from around me, holding his wrist in front of me. Dad always wore a watch, even though most people these days tell time using their phones. I looked at it and my heart sank.

"It's four a.m.," I said. "That's not . . . that's not enough time."

"No," Dad said calmly. "It's not. But here's the thing—it's been four a.m. since we finished the platform."

I squirmed around to look at him, and he nodded. "Yeah. And listen—it hasn't stopped. You can hear it ticking."

I learned forward to press my ear to his wrist, and I heard it, that steady, reassuring tick of time moving forward . . . but not.

"How?" I whispered. I looked toward Koa, who met my gaze steadily, but said nothing.

Dad kissed my temple. "I don't know. But I do know we've still got lots to do, and apparently the time we need to do it all. Ready to get back to work?"

I nodded. Dad gave me a final squeeze and then pulled me back to my feet.

CHAPTER TWENTY

I DON'T KNOW HOW LONG THAT NIGHT LASTED. BUT thanks, I believed, to the magic of the menehune, sunrise held off until the moment that we placed the final rocks atop the walls of the heiau. And as the sun rose, Koa, Hōkū, and Kuawa vanished into the shadows of the forest once more.

We were all exhausted and bleary-eyed, and no one was in any shape to drive. I stumbled along the path, tripping over tree roots and other obstacles that hadn't bothered me in the dark, the light from the rising sun gray and indistinct.

I fell asleep on Puʻulena's shoulder as we rode home in the back seat, with Naomi leaning against the window on my other side. I didn't even know whose car it was. Mom and Dad beat us home, but just barely, and we all mumbled at one another before falling into our respective beds. I kicked off my filthy jeans and slept in my T-shirt, not even bothering to wash my face or brush my teeth.

I regretted that decision when I woke up, but the scent of freshly brewed coffee would soon cover up the smell of my breath. I stumbled out to find Naomi, Puʻulena, and my dad hunched over their mugs of coffee and bowls of cereal, trying to wake up while my mom bustled about the kitchen.

"Good morning, sunshine!" she sang. "Lots to do today!"

I stared at her. "How much coffee have you had, Mom?"

My dad pulled the coffeepot toward himself protectively. "Too much," he muttered.

"Only one cup," she said dismissively.

"That she refilled an unconfirmed number of times," my sister added quietly.

"At least four," Naomi said.

My mom put her hands on her hips. "You guys. We have a wedding *tomorrow*. *Your* wedding, I might add," she said, flicking my sister's shoulder. "We've been working for weeks to get ready. This is the final push! We can do it!"

"Yes," my dad said. "After I eat my cereal."

I hastily went to get myself a bowl before I got assigned a task. There was barely enough in the coffeepot for even my mostly milk coffee, and Puʻulena got up to grind more beans for another batch. We had an old-fashioned hand grinder, useful for those times when the power would go out during storms, and the familiar, loud clanging was a comfort.

Dad leaned back in his chair, and it creaked as he stretched. "All right, Victoria," he said. "What's first?"

"Well, you wanted to make *all* that haupia," she said. "It'll need several hours to chill, and we don't have room for all of that in the refrigerator."

"Danny said there's room at the store. He cleaned out one of the reach-ins for us. And yes, he's set aside plenty of ice."

"Oh!" my mom said. "Well, that's a relief. We've still got to make it, though."

"I can do that," Naomi said. "You've got a recipe, right? Um. What is it?"

"It's coconut pudding . . . sort of," I said, laughing. "Maybe more like creamy coconut Jell-O? I'll show you. It's really easy. Lots of stirring."

"And then we have to set up the tent in case it rains, and then string lights in the tent. And set up tables and chairs. And someone needs to run to Hilo to get the sound equipment for the music, and then tomorrow morning to go pick up the catering . . . plus we have to decorate. And set up coolers with drinks. And put out silverware and plates . . . and oh, God, I have to make the wedding cake!" My mom had been listing her tasks fairly calmly, but when she got to the wedding cake, her voice rose in panic.

My dad sighed heavily and began putting on his shoes. "I'll need help with the tent."

"On it," Puʻulena said.

"Do you need help with the cake, Mom?"

"No!" Mom said. "I just need to be able to concentrate. I have this new fondant recipe, it's supposed to actually taste good, but I haven't made it before, so—"

I tugged on Naomi's hand and pulled her out of the kitchen. "We'll go make the haupia at my uncle's store," I said.

After going our separate ways for a few hours—and getting the haupia into the refrigerators—we reconvened to get the tent set up. It was one of those big white things with scalloped edges and enough space for everyone to fit underneath. It wasn't supposed to rain tomorrow, but this was Hawai'i, so who knew? The grass was still squishy damp from the downpour early yesterday evening—was it really only just yesterday?—but it was drying in the sun and hopefully wouldn't get too muddy.

I thought the tents we put up when we went camping were complicated, but this one required so much more coordination of people all moving at once. Following my dad's instructions, I lifted when he told me to lift, and hammered stakes where he told me to hammer them. My muscles ached from the labors of the night before, but, well, as my mom said, the wedding was tomorrow. There was nothing else to be done, and we were all feeling it. We ate chips and salsa for lunch while sitting in the grass, too tired to talk.

And so it went. Once one task was completed, there was always another, as we taped white paper to the folding tables, lū'au-style, and hung white crepe bunting along the sides of the tent. We set up the speakers and stereo once my auntie dropped them off on her way home from Hilo, and we put a smaller tent up over them, too, just in case.

I peeked into the kitchen occasionally, checking on my mom's progress with the cake. It was multitiered. Let no one say she didn't work well under pressure.

I tried to figure out if Puʻulena or Naomi was nervous, but it didn't seem like it. Probably they were just too tired. Maybe nervous would come tomorrow.

We didn't bother with a traditional rehearsal dinner—after all, there was nothing to rehearse. Nobody was doing readings or anything complicated. You walk to a place, you say a few things, you kiss, everybody claps. Instead, we went to dinner at the Thai restaurant (the one my sister used to wash dishes at, obviously) and ordered half the menu and lilikoi margaritas for all (nonalcoholic for me), and everyone told embarrassing stories about Puʻulena and talked over one another and laughed until the owner told us we had to go home already.

As I was heading into my bedroom to go to sleep, my sister stopped me with a hand on my shoulder. "Emma, tell me the truth. Do you hate your bridesmaid dress?"

"No!" I protested. "Not at all."

"I know you like pink . . . ," she said.

"But you hate it," I finished. "Your wedding was *never* going to feature a pink dress, Puʻulena. And I *love* my blue dress. I promise."

"Okay. But, you know, I wanted to make it up to you. And I think you're supposed to give bridesmaid gifts, right? Isn't that a thing? So anyway, here, I got this for you." She handed me a little brown paper bag, and inside was a box with a gorgeous gold bracelet, etched with my Hawaiian name, Kanilehua, the rain that falls onto the blossoms of the ʻōhiʻa trees.

I gasped aloud. "Puʻulena! This is so beautiful! You didn't need to do this!"

She wrapped an arm around my shoulders and hugged me tight. "And you didn't need to be so great. But you are."

I would be lying if I said I didn't cry. Or that I didn't pet my bracelet several times while brushing my teeth and getting ready for bed.

But I couldn't sleep. I was exhausted. I should have been incapable of not sleeping, but rest just wouldn't come. I kept feeling like there was something I hadn't done, some task I'd left unfinished, and no amount of reminding myself that I had plenty of time tomorrow to figure out what it was and take care of it was doing any good whatsoever.

Finally, I threw back the blankets and stood up. I desperately needed to get to sleep, and if going over any potential incomplete tasks was what it was going to take, then that was what I was going to do.

I stepped into my mom's work boots, which were too big, but I could put them on easily and they would keep my feet dry in the dew-wet grass. I pulled on a jacket and grabbed a flashlight. I doubted I still had my ability to see in the dark—and yes, once I got outside, I definitely needed it, even with the relatively clear moonlit sky. I made my way through the darkness to where the white tent stood like an oversized mushroom that had just sprouted up on the lawn. I ran my hand across the white-papered tables. The paper was a little damp from the moist air but would be crisp enough once the sun came out in the morning.

I couldn't see anything that had been left undone, nothing that didn't have to wait until tomorrow anyway. I sighed heavily and rubbed the back of my hand over my eyes. They were burning with exhaustion again, and I had that sore throat that happens when I didn't get enough rest. I turned to head back to the house and found Koa standing before me. I hadn't heard him make a sound.

He just stood there looking at me for a long moment. His face, always so fierce, was more difficult to read than ever. At last, he spoke. "Emma, I need you to kneel."

I did, shuffling awkwardly in my mother's boots as I lowered myself down to the grass, the wet soaking through my pajama pants. On my knees, I could look Koa in the eye. He stepped forward and pressed his heavy brow to mine, bringing our noses to touch, his arms gripping my shoulders. We inhaled and exhaled together, exchanging hā, our breath—our life.

"We owe you a debt," Koa said, stepping back.

I shook my head. "There is no debt, Koa. Just—is everyone going to be all right? Will you be able to find a new cave to live in?"

"We already have. We are moving the young ones and supplies as we speak. There is a lava tube close by the heiau; did you know that? It's new and smooth and strong. It is a good home for us."

I sat back on the heels of my too-large boots, sagging with relief. "Oh. Oh, thank goodness."

"You were right. That forest needs us. It needs rain and life. We have lived here, in this old forest, for so long. We forgot what it is to tend a forest through its rebirth. But I will miss it here, and I will miss you, Emma Arruda. Take care of this forest for me."

I swallowed past the lump in my throat. "I will. I promise."

CHAPTER TWENTY-ONE

THE MORNING OF THE WEDDING DAWNED bright and warm. It was the rare kind of day in Volcano when everything seems to be brighter, more vibrant, than anywhere else. The sky bluer, the trees greener, the air clean and sparkling. On days like that, there is nowhere else on earth that could possibly compare.

I like to think it was a gift from the menehune. Or maybe it was just the trade winds doing their job, clearing out the rain, at least for a little while.

There was a lot to do. Eventually my mom yelled at Puʻulena and Naomi to stop whatever they were doing and go get ready, for crying out loud. Naomi's family had flown in that morning and were doing their best to follow my mom's chaotic and sometimes contradictory instructions (*she* was definitely nervous). I think the centerpieces on the tables got moved a total of eleven times.

At last, there was nothing else to be done, and I hurried to go get dressed myself. I had lied to Puʻulena, a little bit—the dress was pretty, even though it wasn't pink, but I wasn't completely comfortable in it. It was strapless, and, well, I wasn't sure I had what it took to hold it up. The Arruda women were busty, but they were also slow to get there.

But when I tried it on this time, I felt different. My boobs definitely weren't bigger, but my shoulders were straighter. I stood up taller.

I climbed on top of the toilet so I could see the dress in the mirror over the sink (full-length mirrors being in short supply at the moment), and I looked . . . elegant. The blue was a dark, powdery indigo, and it flared out like a bell at my waist. I pinned the spray of 'iwa'iwa ferns and pīkake blossoms behind my ear, their fragrance clean and sweet. There was no way I could manage heels in the grass, even thick stacked ones, but I did wear my dressy slippers. And it's possible I was imagining things, but I thought my biceps looked pretty ripped after all that rock hauling.

When I went to Pu'ulena and Naomi's room, my mom was there, freaking out, of course. Auntie Carol poked her head in, took one look at the situation, and came back with a glass of wine, plus the bottle. "Victoria, relax," she said. "Everything is wonderful."

"That's what I've been trying to tell her!" Pu'ulena said. I finally got a good look at her, and she took my breath away. Normally, Pu'ulena dressed, well, sort of sporty—big hoop earrings were her only real concession to my much more girly sense of style. But today was her wedding day. Her dress was from Sig Zane, the Big Island aloha wear designer of choice. It was simple but elegant, with his traditional clean lines and cotton fabric, with a light-blue-on-white 'iwa'iwa print. Her hair was down, hanging long and straight.

By contrast, Naomi's dress was vintage and lacy, with a train that she was absolutely going to spend the whole night tripping on, but it didn't matter—she was a giggling, joyful vision, and I loved them both so much I couldn't stand it.

The glass of wine seemed to be having its intended effect, and Mom calmed down enough to stand still for photos. And then, soon enough, the appointed time arrived, and Puʻulena and Naomi stepped out, ready to walk arm in arm down the shell-lined aisle.

"Wait!" Auntie Carol came rushing over. "You can't start yet. Uncle Mike isn't here!"

"What?" my mom snapped. "Where is he?"

"He had to go home and get dressed. He was here until five minutes ago, but there was an issue with the lights in the tent, and he had to fix it, and then he had to go get ready. He'll be here in five minutes; I promise."

I peeked around the corner of the house at the crowd standing out on the lawn. Every one of my relatives was there, which was a big party all in itself, plus friends and neighbors, Puʻulena's friends from high school, Naomi's family, and a few friends who had flown out (it is a long way, after all). Ana was there with her parents, and I could see that Puʻulena must have invited the Kaneshiros, because there was Hilo. He wasn't wearing a suit or anything, but he'd tucked a dress shirt into his jeans and rolled up the cuffs of his sleeves against the warmth of the afternoon sun.

He looked nice.

As if he felt my eyes on him, he glanced my way, and his face lit up with a smile. He waved, and I felt myself blushing as I waved back.

We went back inside to enjoy another glass of wine—I had a small ceremonial glass—and waited relatively patiently for the signal that Uncle Mike was back and we were ready to go. At last, we heard the strains of "Ke Kali Nei Au" and scrambled out the door, with Naomi tripping over her train, of course.

I went first, walking to the incredibly slow beat of the song. I felt everyone's eyes on me and blushed, but my shoulders stayed straight. When I reached the top of the hill, I moved aside, allowing Puʻulena and Naomi to stand side by side in front of Judge Keawe, a family friend I'd known my whole life.

I didn't really pay attention to what he said. I was busy watching everyone watching my sister, watching my mom try not to cry, watching my dad definitely crying, watching my aunts and uncles and cousins and friends standing in the sunlight, watching Puʻulena and Naomi absolutely beaming at each other, radiating a light brighter even than the sun.

Judge Keawe was just getting to the really important questions part when there was a commotion at the back of the crowd, and Mālie, who had been locked up in the garage for the event, came tearing up the hill. Naomi shrieked, and Puʻulena knelt so as not to get jumped on, and I rushed over to tug Mālie away, to come stand with me and be a doggy bridesmaid, and everyone was laughing, and suddenly there was even more joy, which I didn't think was possible. Judge Keawe rushed through the rest of the ceremony, and Naomi bent Puʻulena back in a dramatic kiss, and I'm pretty sure by that point I was crying, too.

I watched Puʻulena dancing with Naomi, the twinkle lights Uncle Mike had strung overhead sparkling like brighter stars. It was a Springsteen song, of all things, but then Puʻulena had always loved Bruce, and Naomi must have really loved her to go along with this for their first dance. A few of my youngest cousins and a couple of other little kids I couldn't fully identify were circling around them, blowing bubbles, but they seemed totally unaware, just swaying together, not even smiling, their arms wrapped around each other.

I felt someone come up from behind to stand next to me. I didn't have to look to know it was Hilo. His shoulder brushed up against mine, his shirt crisp against my bare shoulder. The sun had gone down, and I should have been feeling cold, but I wasn't. Too much excitement, maybe. Or too much fruit punch. (It's possible the fruit punch might have been the teensiest bit spiked.)

"It feels weird, knowing that they aren't here," he said.

I knew what he meant. A little of the magic had left Volcano, magic that I had felt my whole life, without even realizing it. The other spirits were still there, of course—I could see an owl in the trees and feel the 'ōhi'a watching us, benevolently this time. And I knew that, with the menehune gone, it was now my job—our job—to watch over the forest, as they had done for so long. I didn't know how we would do it, what we could possibly do to prevent the changes that were always coming, always insistent and inexorable. But maybe not inevitable.

Hilo took my hand, and I squeezed his fingers. He tugged a little, and I turned to look at him. He reached up with his other hand, cupping my head gently. I knew what he was going to do one moment before he did it.

I'd kissed other boys before. Well, one boy. Ikaika and I had kissed a bunch when we'd dated for those three months. But with Hilo's mouth on mine, it really didn't feel like that had counted. I was conscious of the lights, of all the people, of my parents and Hilo's parents and everyone else. I could taste the coconut haupia he'd had for dessert, sweet and soft, and beneath that, the taste of *him*, at his core. I wondered if he could taste me beneath the fruit punch.

And then I stopped thinking, stopped wondering, and put my arms around him, my lost boy from the forest.

When he pulled back, I was shaking and breathless. He grinned and kissed me once more, quickly, then tugged at the hand he was still holding. "Come dance with me."

Springsteen had ended, thank heavens, and my dad was grabbing my mom, and she was protesting, but it was clearly only for show. Naomi was laughing as her father spun her around in some pretty impressive swing-dance moves. Ana and her mom and dad had some kind of three-person jig going, and Puʻulena was looking at me with an *Oooooooh* face that I firmly ignored. And then Hilo was spinning me this way and that, and I know for sure that I definitely did not look as cool as Naomi doing it, but I looked up at the stars as I spun, knowing that Hilo would catch me if I fell.

And then, in the shadows of the trees, outside the circle of strung lights, I saw him. Koa, standing at the edge of the forest. He had come all this way. I gripped Hilo's shoulder, and he followed my gaze. Koa bowed his head, and we bowed back.

EPILOGUE

I may or may not have drunk more fruit punch that night. I definitely kissed Hilo several more times. Mālie had brought Snookie as her date, and the two of them got into the cake, but thankfully only after it had been cut and admired, otherwise I think my mom might have had a breakdown. Ana and I perfected our impressions of those floppy guys you see at car dealerships, and Puʻulena and I did a dance-off that, contrary to all other opinions, I definitely won. I don't remember going to bed. I think we were all in a fugue state of excitement and exhaustion.

    I dragged my eyes open in the dawn light and groaned. If the setup for the wedding had been bad, the takedown would be worse, and I'd promised Mom that I'd help first thing in the morning so that Puʻulena and Naomi could leave for their honeymoon on Kauaʻi without feeling guilty. I pulled on a sweatshirt and jeans, reminding myself that weddings are only once and it was definitely about to be over and also it was extremely fun and romantic and I loved Puʻulena and Naomi and I would do anything for them, absolutely including cleaning up a big party at six thirty in the morning.

    I closed the door behind me softly, hoping to let everyone else sleep a bit longer if they could. The dew on the grass was cold on my slippered feet. I rounded the corner of the house and gaped.

The lights had been taken down and were neatly coiled at the base of a tree. The tent had been dismantled. The chairs and tables had been folded. The trash was gone. All that was left were Puʻulena and Naomi's bouquets, placed carefully atop the hill, at the end of the rows of shells.

I smiled. "Thank you, Koa," I whispered, though I knew he had gone. I leaned down to pick up the flowers, then ran my hand over the rough gray bark of the nearby ʻōhiʻa tree. In a few hours, Puʻulena would leave for her honeymoon. In a few weeks, I'd be back at school, seeing Ana every day and maybe Hilo, too. Work would start up again at the back of Wright Road, and one day, in all likelihood, it probably would end up being a resort and Volcano would change. But I would do what I could, taking care of what I could manage, protecting my home and the place I loved. And I would keep my eyes on the invisible wild, the intangible space where two worlds meet, where the possible touches the impossible.

AUTHOR'S NOTE

This is fiction. But it's also not. I've done my best to write about my childhood, my experience growing up in Hawaiʻi. I think everyone writing about an underrepresented culture feels a sense of panic, because we all know that our experience isn't universal, and I know that the Hawaiʻi I'm writing about here isn't the one that most people envision or experience. This isn't meant to represent Hawaiian culture in its entirety—that would be impossible. It's just meant to give a single facet.

Issues of cultural and environmental preservation, Native Hawaiian self-determinism, agriculture, industry, tourism, land use, Hawaiian sovereignty, the 2023 disaster on Maui, and the ongoing controversy on Mauna Kea are far more complex than I have made them seem here. This is the perspective of a relatively sheltered sixteen-year-old, and I would encourage everyone to dive into these issues as, no matter where you live, these questions involve us all.

The legends of menehune have always been a source of curiosity and wonder, and this shifted interpretation is by no means representative of those legends, but is instead a result of imagining what menehune would be like today, as a marginalized culture. Similarly, the menehune heiau described isn't the traditional Hawaiian cultural heiau, but something I thought the menehune might have built for the culture I imagined for them based on their folklore.

That said, so much of this is true, and I hope my family sees the love I have for them here on the page, as well as the love I have for my home and my culture.

ACKNOWLEDGMENTS

Writing acknowledgments here feels impossible, because how do you thank people for your whole life? Nevertheless, I have to thank my mom, who always wants me to see the hidden things; my dad, who always knows how to take a hard situation and make it easier; and Hannah (How about this AU where you're the big sister? Do you think we'd have gotten along better? Love you). Thank you to David and Puanani, as well as my aunties, uncles, cousins, and friends, and my incredible town. I have to thank Nina Yuen, who was there from the very beginning and ever shall be, and Mrs. Sheila Watson, the kindest and most generous teacher a little girl could have, who handed me Madeleine L'Engle and Tamora Pierce and told me I could do something like that.

I am eternally grateful to my agent and friend, Sara Crowe, for never yet giving up on me, and for telling me (long, long ago) that I had a voice for children's fiction. Thank you so much to my editor, Allison Cohen, who understood what I wanted to do with this book and helped me get it there, who values and believes in the same things I do. I am so, so happy we got to do this together. Thank you to the illustrator, Carolina Rodriguez Fuenmayor, for an *absolute beauty* of a cover. I don't think I can write a book without thanking Shannon Fabricant (I haven't yet!)—Shannon, I am eternally grateful to you. Thank you to Frances Soo Ping Chow for her always wonderful design, to Amber Morris, Jess Riordan, and Lindsay Ricketts for tracking everything and always being so wonderfully cheery and careful about "So *which* way does the 'okina curve?" And enormous thanks to Sarah Chassé for being such a careful and badass copy editor—I'm in awe. To the entire wonderful team at Running Press—you're the best and have always been the best and will always be the best. I thank my lucky stars every day for you.

I have to thank Annie Nichol for being my writing partner, editor, and bosom friend, and Alex Parker for answering geological questions and general hand-holding. Thank you to Lenora, Linh, and Bel, the War Scribes who jumped in with thoughts, feedback, writing encouragement, and, of course, rants. I have to thank Kahua, for always offering me translations for 'Ōlelo Hawai'i, always researching mo'olelo, and always, always being supportive and generally an inspiration. And Dave, who sits with me as I write and gives instant feedback, encouraging me to write a story I didn't think I had the right to tell. I love you all.